'It's surprising how many people there are in th... ...er to stay unco...

Katie nodded. 'Y...'

Tim's smile broadened. 'But what would you do if someone tried to cast his wicked spell over you again?'

'I wouldn't let it happen! Romantic love isn't for me any more. I'm a clear-headed, hard-working professional woman and I can live without it. I mean, who needs it?'

Margaret Barker pursued a variety of interesting careers before she became a full-time author. Besides holding a BA degree in French and Linguistics, she is a Licentiate of the Royal Academy of Music, a State Registered Nurse and a qualified teacher. Happily married, she has two sons, a daughter, and an increasing number of grandchildren. She lives with her husband in a sixteenth-century thatched house near the East Anglian coast.

Recent titles by the same author:

CAROL'S CHRISTMAS
HERO'S LEGACY
HOME-COMING

VALENTINE MAGIC

BY
MARGARET BARKER

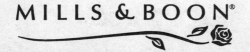

MILLS & BOON®

First published in Great Britain 1998
Harlequin Mills & Boon Limited,
Eton House, 18-24 Paradise Road, Richmond, Surrey TW9 1SR

© Margaret Barker 1998

ISBN 0 263 81419 X

Set in Times Roman 10½ on 12 pt.
03-9902-49362-D

Printed and bound in Norway
by AIT Trondheim AS, Trondheim

CHAPTER ONE

KATIE took another sip of the refreshingly chilled orange juice which she'd discovered in the fridge of her thatched water bungalow on stilts over the sea, before leaning back against the cushions of the cane armchair. The powerful rays of the sun were already pointing fingers towards the wide expanse of iridescent sea directly in front of her veranda and illuminating the sky with a magical shade of pink that was rapidly turning to gold.

'Mmm!' she remarked to the shoal of blue surgeon fish, cavorting leisurely in front of and underneath her veranda. 'I could get used to this!'

One of the plump, royal blue, black-headed, yellow-finned fish seemed to turn its head to look at her, probably hoping for a nibble of something. The previous occupant of her water bungalow was sure to have fed the fish. How could you not feed them when they swarmed past in dazzlingly spectacular shoals which you felt you wanted to reach out and touch?

She must remember to bring some bread over from the dining room after supper, though these fish were certainly not starving by the look of their plump, well-rounded bodies!

Katie glanced down at the fish guide that she'd bought in the island shop soon after arriving, proud of the fact that she'd been able to identify the blue surgeon fish.

Nice of these fish to welcome her to her temporary home, and how appropriate that they should have been given a medical-sounding name! She hoped when she met up with the surgeon in charge of the medical facilities in this group of Maldive islands she would find him as welcoming and easy to get on with.

Half a dozen yellow parrot fish swam into view, one of them jumping, obligingly, out of the sea to snap at a dragonfly, giving her a much better view of its shimmering scales.

Katie sighed again in utter contentment. This place really was paradise on earth as described in all the travel brochures she'd ever studied.

A chill memory suddenly forced itself upon her, dispersing some of the magic as she remembered the first time she'd seen a brochure about the Maldives. It had been the night the Rat had taken her to that fancy restaurant near the hospital on one of her rare evenings off from working as a junior house surgeon. He'd asked her to marry him and she, like an idiot, had agreed.

As he'd spread the brochures on the starched white linen tablecloth, she'd been thrilled at the prospect of a honeymoon on one of these spectacular islands.

'Only problem is, which one?' he'd drawled, in that bored, I've-been-everywhere, phoney voice that she should have seen through, his hand squeezing hers.

How could she have been so stupid, such a bad judge of character? What had it been about Rick's personality that had drawn her towards him? Why had she felt as if she'd been under some kind of spell? How on earth had she imagined she wanted to spend the rest of her life with him? Had the lure of the Maldivian island honeymoon addled her brain?

Enough of this depressing introspection! She'd made it under her own steam now—taken a six-month assignment. When she wasn't on duty she would have time to explore the islands, without the Rat breathing down her neck—as he would most certainly have done. He'd been so possessive—until he'd run off with someone else.

The sound of a small seaplane approaching the island broke into her thoughts. It was coming in from the direction of Male, the capital of the Maldives. This would be the surgeon in charge. She'd been told to expect him around sunset when he'd finished his work in the main hospital.

She watched the distinctive red, white and black plane swooping down, preparing to land on the sea. Behind it, the sun had almost disappeared into the water, the lower half of the flaming sphere hanging heavily above the smooth, silkily shiny horizon as it prepared to sink without trace into the intractable depths of the sea.

The plane skidded on its floats, spraying a shower of water behind it as it skimmed the surface and came to a halt only yards from the shore by the side of the wooden landing platform. A lone figure, his head bathed in the flaming glow of the sunset, came down the steps, crossed the small platform and stepped into the waiting boat, which she'd learned only today as she'd come across from the airport was called a *dhoni*.

Almost immediately, the plane's propellers spun into action again as the pilot taxied back through the channel between the coral reefs, before flying off towards the dying rays of the sun.

If this was Dr Tim Fielding, her new boss, then it looked as if he was going to stay the night on the island. Good! That would give her time to ask all the questions that were buzzing in her brain. It would also mean she could ask his advice about the young girl who was waiting to have her baby in the little hospital close by.

The day sister in charge had assured Katie, during her brief visit to the hospital, that there was nothing the nurs-

ing staff couldn't handle, and that she should go and
settle into her bungalow. But while she'd been taking in
the beauty of her new surroundings she'd found her
mind flitting back to the young patient and wondering if
she should go back for a final check.

The mother-to-be was only sixteen, very tiny and very
frail. Surrounded by the various women of her family—
mother, aunts, grandmother—she had looked up at Katie
with soulful, resigned-to-her-fate eyes, but underneath
the placid exterior Katie had sensed she was scared stiff.
Katie planned to go back just as soon as she'd met Dr
Fielding, and hoped that the night sister wasn't as unsympathetic as the day sister.

Perhaps 'unsympathetic' was too strong a word for
the hard-working sister who'd shown her round the small
hospital with great pride. It had been obvious that she'd
wanted to impress on Katie that she could run the hospital single-handed if necessary and that Katie's appointment as doctor in the area had been totally unnecessary.

Apparently, they'd managed without a doctor in residence before her arrival, simply calling in one of the
doctors from the Indira Gandhi hospital in Male for dire
emergencies or transferring the patient there for in-
patient hospital care.

Looking out over the wooden railing of her veranda,
poised over the sea, she could see that the approaching
doctor was now sprinting along the white sand towards
her bungalow, which was the first building of a group
of six. She went inside and crossed the polished, wood
block floor of her sitting room to the front door.

Opening it, she watched as the tall figure of her new
boss slowed his pace to cross the wooden walkway over
the narrow stretch of swirling blue sea that separated her
bungalow from the island beach.

'Tim Fielding,' he said, stretching out his hand towards her.

Strong, firm fingers folded around hers as she looked up into a pair of startlingly blue eyes. His dark hair was falling over his face and he removed his hand to brush a couple of strands from his line of vision.

'Katie Mandrake,' she said, stepping backwards into the room as Dr Fielding towered above her, filling the entire doorway.

'I need to stretch my legs after being cooped up in Theatre all day,' he said in a deep, gravelly voice as he strode past her. 'When we've had a preliminary chat I'll have a run round the island.'

He was walking briskly across her room, making for the veranda where the final crimson tip of the sun could be seen disappearing into the sea.

Oh, not another sports freak! she thought, her heart sinking.

Looking at the broad back as it disappeared through the casement windows, she could almost imagine that it was the Rat! He had the same athletic shape, his well-honed muscles standing out against the thin cotton of his shirt—obviously a man who took his exercise very seriously.

Still, it didn't affect her in any way. What Dr Tim Fielding did with his off-duty time was no concern of hers. As long as he didn't expect her to listen to how long it had taken him to run round the island and how he'd knocked three whole seconds from his previous onslaught on the land speed record, she—

'Got anything to drink?' he called, as he sank into one of the cane chairs.

'Orange juice OK?'

'Perfect.'

As she opened the fridge she noticed various bottles stacked behind the orange juice. There were miniature bottles of gin, whisky, a couple of bottles of beer, various mixers and even a bottle of champagne. Such luxury! Her own fridge, back in the tiny London flat she'd rented, had rarely contained anything more exotic than a wilting lettuce and a couple of tomatoes.

'You can have something stronger, if you prefer, Dr Fielding,' she called, addressing the broad back she could see through the full-length casement window. He'd closed the glass doors to conserve the air conditioning in her room and she had to shout to make herself heard.

'Just orange juice,' she thought she heard him reply with a perfunctory wave of the hand, and she made her way back to the veranda.

She handed over the glass of orange juice, which he drank in one fell swoop, placing the empty glass on the circular cane drinks table.

'Would you like another one?'

He smiled, an easy movement of the lips that spread to his captivatingly expressive blue eyes, helping to remove her feeling that she was simply playing waitress to a self-important boss, hell-bent on making sure she knew her place.

'Yes, please, and maybe just a dash of soda to spice it up. Got to keep up our fluid intake out here. One and a half litres of bottled mineral water a day at least. Don't forget that, will you, Dr Mandrake?'

Returning to the sitting room, she pulled a comical face at the open fridge.

'I'll try not to forget your advice,' she called, as she poured out another glass of orange juice, 'spicing it', as the boss had ordered, with a hint of soda and taking the remaining soda in the can out onto the veranda.

'Best part of the day,' he said, his voice more relaxed than before, as he stretched long, cotton chino-clad legs out in front of him. 'Did you go to see the feeding of the sting rays?'

'No, what...?'

'Just before sundown every evening these huge dark grey creatures glide up to the shore, and one of the waiters from the restaurant takes buckets of food out and feeds them by hand. It's a magnificent sight!'

He sounded young and boyish when he was describing something that obviously interested him. She watched him brush a hand through his somewhat unruly hair. How old was he? Thirty-five perhaps, maybe thirty-six? Definitely a few years older than she was.

Katie leaned back against the cushions of her chair. 'I've been settling into my palatial apartment ever since I got back from the hospital. I certainly didn't expect this sort of luxury. How come I've been assigned a bungalow that belongs to the tourist resort and, more importantly, how much do I have to pay towards my food in the restaurant, the contents of the fridge and—?'

'Hang on, hang on!' he said, putting a large hand on the arm of her chair. 'There's no need to worry about money,' he told her, firmly. 'The tour company that owns these bungalows is providing a large percentage of our salaries. We are paid partly by the Maldivian government because of our involvement in the medical care of their people but, basically, the large tour companies can afford to subsidise us in appreciation of the fact that we take care of their clients, for which they are extremely grateful.'

'Well, yes, I'd had that explained at my interview in London, but the contents of the fridge, for instance?'

'A drop in the ocean,' he replied dismissively. 'We take care of the tourist clients; the company takes care of our day-to-day requirements—food, drink, uniforms for the nurses. The cost is negligible where health care is involved.'

'Well, that's a relief!' She put down her empty glass. 'The main problem I've hit since arriving here this afternoon is the lack of co-operation from the nursing staff at the hospital.'

She took a deep breath as she watched the narrowing of his expressive eyes. 'They seemed to think that I was redundant to requirements.'

'Give them time, Dr Mandrake! You've been here a matter of hours. They'll come round when they really need your help. They're not stand-offish with me.'

'Yes, but you're a man!'

'You noticed!'

He laughed, a deep, reverberating, throaty sound that unnerved her. Yes, he certainly was all man, his every movement oozing virility. The sort of man who thought he could run rings around the fairer sex. Just like the Rat!

'What I meant to say,' she hurried on, glad that the darkening sky was concealing her heightened colour, 'was that the nurses seemed as if they resented me being there. And I'm worried about a young patient I saw, waiting to be delivered of her first child. Her name is Fatima. She's so young—only sixteen—and she seemed frightened.'

He was already standing, his handsome, tanned face suddenly serious as he listened to her obvious concern.

He moved to the glass casement window and slid it to one side.

A draught of cold air from the air-conditioned room hit her like a chill north wind, increasing her fears for the patient's welfare.

'Let's go and see her. I know the patient you mean,' he said evenly. 'Is her mother with her?'

They were crossing her sitting room, making their way to the front door. Dr Fielding opened the door, holding it so that she could go out before him.

Automatically, she felt in the pocket of her cotton dress. Yes, the bungalow key was still there. She didn't want to lock herself out, although with the number of helpful room boys and domestic helpers on hand she doubted she would have to wait long to be let in with a master key.

It was unnerving to be walking in front of her boss as they crossed the wooden walkway from the bungalow to the beach. She was very much aware of his towering presence as she answered his questions about their patient.

'Yes, Fatima's mother is with her, and her grandmother, not to mention a few aunts, possibly even a sister or two. They were coming and going all the time I was there.'

The warm sand sifted through her open-toed sandals. Earlier in the day, soon after she'd arrived, the sand had been too hot for her bare feet when she'd taken a short swim.

'All the female members of the family are involved in a birth,' Dr Fielding told her as they trekked across the beach towards the lights of the path that led to the small hospital.

'They bring in all the food the patient requires, they

take the prescriptions to the dispensary and, just by being there, they help to reassure the patient.'

'Well, it's going to take some getting used to,' she said quietly.

'Exactly! Keep an open mind and you'll learn as you go along. I presume you had some compelling reason for wanting to work out here in the Maldives?'

Katie swallowed hard. Coming like that, out of the blue, she had no time to prepare her answer. How could she tell Dr Fielding that her compelling reason was to lay the ghost of the Rat? Having taken their joint savings four years ago, he'd absconded here with a new girl-friend for a two-week holiday that should have been their own honeymoon.

However you looked at it, it was not a very philan-thropic or altruistic reason, but something very necessary to her mental and physical well-being. Nevertheless, she intended to throw herself wholeheartedly into using her innate and acquired medical skills to take care of her patients.

'I've always wanted to come here,' she began halt-ingly. 'When I read about the position of doctor, based on Kamafaroo island for six months, I felt it was too good to miss.'

She glanced up in the twilight and could see that Dr Fielding was smiling, his eyes crinkling attractively.

'At least you didn't give the stock reply that you felt it was a challenge.' He hesitated. 'Do I get the impres-sion that there's another reason you're holding back on?'

Was she so transparent, or was this man, in spite of her initial impression, highly sensitive?

'There is a reason, but...but I don't want to talk about it...at least not just now.'

Why had she said that? Why hadn't she just knocked

his curiosity on the head? What had it to do with him, anyway? He was only her boss. Her personal life shouldn't be his concern.

'OK, fair enough. But if you ever feel the need to unburden yourself, I've got a sympathetic ear and I do take the welfare of my staff very seriously. If something's worrying you...'

'Thank you, it's not,' she said abruptly, wishing fervently that she'd kept her mouth shut.

They were passing between the small, round, thatched-roof houses on either side of the sandy path leading to the wooden building that was the centre of the medical facilities for Kamafaroo and the surrounding islands. Grouped around the open doors of the little houses, mothers and children sat in the welcoming cool of the evening, chatting and laughing.

Their inherent easygoing happiness was infectious. Katie smiled and waved to a couple of small toddlers, playing in the sand. They smiled and waved back as she approached the hospital. Above the main entrance a light above the painted sign indicated that this was Kamafaroo Hospital.

Tim Fielding pushed open the door, which was heavily screened with mesh to keep out the flies and other insects that were drawn to the light after nightfall. A young Maldivian nurse in a white cotton uniform dress, her black, shiny hair falling down her back to her tiny waist in a becoming, thick, braided plait, got up from the desk beside the door.

What a beautiful hairstyle! Simple, yet sophisticated. Katie wondered fleetingly if she could copy it with her own long brown hair. But would she ever be able to achieve that intense gloss? It looked like something from those shampoo adverts on TV.

When she was twenty-one, her mother had suggested it was time to have her long hair cut into 'something more suitable', especially as she'd been training to be a doctor and needed to look professional. But she'd resisted the idea and continued to tie her hair back with a ribbon, sometimes confining it in a chignon, like today, when she needed to give a good impression.

Soon after her twenty-ninth birthday earlier this year, after a weekend with her mother, she'd actually got herself to the hairdresser with a request for a short, chic cut. But at the last moment, with the scissors poised above her, she'd asked the stylist to stop.

Moving her hand, surreptitiously, to the back of her neck, she checked if the pins of the chignon were still in place. Only just!

'What a pleasant surprise, Dr Fielding,' the nurse was saying, now standing in front of the desk, her neck craned to an angle whereby she could look up towards his face. 'I didn't know you were coming this evening or I would—'

'That's OK, Nurse Sabia—just a passing visit to introduce my colleague, Dr Katie Mandrake.'

The corners of the nurse's mouth twitched into an approximation of a smile.

'Yes, I met Dr Mandrake earlier this afternoon when Sister Habaid showed her round the hospital.'

'You've had a long day, Nurse,' Katie said, smiling sympathetically. 'What time do the night staff take over?'

'Some of them are here already, but the day staff remain until everything has been finished to the satisfaction of Sister Habaid.'

I'm sure they do! Katie thought. She couldn't help but admire such exemplary devotion to duty.

'We're going to Obstetrics,' Dr Fielding said, moving away from the desk.

'Would you like me to accompany you, Doctor?' Nurse Sabia said.

Tim Fielding smiled as he shook his head. 'No need, Nurse. I'm sure you have work to do here.'

They walked along the narrow corridor together. Through the open doors of the small wards Katie could see numerous relatives crowding round the beds of their loved ones.

'It's a very good system,' Dr Fielding said. 'It certainly eases the workload for the nurses. We could do with something like this in the UK.'

'I don't think it would work,' Katie said.

She saw her boss's eyebrows shoot up.

'Why not?'

'In the UK relatives are too busy with their own lives to spend hours waiting around the hospital.'

He stroked his chin, an enigmatic expression in his perceptive blue eyes. 'And you approve of that, do you?'

'I neither approve nor disapprove. I'm simply pointing out...'

She paused. Was he trying to provoke an argument or simply winding her up? Fortunately, they'd reached a door with 'Obstetrics' written over it so she was able to keep her opinions to herself.

The plump little sister that Katie had met earlier in the day came bustling up to the door, smoothing capable hands over the white cotton of her uniform dress, her face wreathed in smiles as she looked up at Dr Fielding.

'Hello, Sister, we've come to see how Fatima is getting on.'

'No problem, Doctor,' Sister Habaid said. 'Our young mother will be delivered before morning.'

'Well, let's take a look, shall we?'

As Katie followed Tim Fielding and Sister Habaid further down the ward she had the distinct impression that she was being excluded. Or was jet lag taking over and making her unnecessarily sensitive? Still, all she was concerned about was the welfare of the young girl whose pleading eyes had disturbed her earlier in the day.

'We have taken Fatima to our delivery room,' Sister said, pushing open double doors at the end of the ward.

Bright lights hit Katie so that after the dim interior of the ward it took a couple of seconds for her eyes to focus on the small, pathetic figure stretched out on the delivery table.

'How long has Fatima been in the delivery room, Sister?' Katie asked quietly.

Sister Habaid glanced at a chart secured to the end of the delivery table. 'Four hours so it won't be long before she is delivered.'

Katie moved to the table, smiling at her patient as she placed practised hands over the young girl's abdomen. 'How frequent are the contractions, Sister?'

Again, the sister consulted Fatima's notes. 'They were very frequent until an hour ago. For some time now they have been less frequent and...'

The Sister's voice droned on but Katie had turned her full attention on the patient, who was quietly withdrawn, her face lined with anxiety.

Katie removed her hand from the contractionless abdomen and took Fatima's hand in hers. She felt the tiny fingers latch onto hers as if to a lifeline. The four female relatives moved closer, watching Katie with wary eyes.

Katie looked up at Tim Fielding and saw the concerned expression in his eyes. 'Do you agree that we should speed things up, Doctor?' she asked him under her breath.

He nodded. 'I'll fix up a drip with something to get the contractions going again while you check just how far on Fatima actually is.' He lowered his voice. 'She would prefer a lady doctor to do the more intimate examination.'

'Do you think we could dispense with the audience?' Katie whispered.

'I think that could be arranged,' he replied, before giving brief instructions to Sister Habaid.

The sister was frowning as she explained to the relatives that the doctors wanted to clear the room. One by one they disappeared back into the ward, and as they did so Katie was relieved to see the briefest of smiles cross her patient's lips.

'I'm not surprised the poor girl was all tense, having to produce her first child under full view of everybody,' she said quietly, as she handed Tim Fielding a sterile pack to fix up the drip on Fatima.

'It's customary in the village where she was born,' he said quietly. 'We can't fly in the face of tradition.'

'We can in the case of an emergency,' Katie told him, surprising herself by her boldness towards her boss. 'This poor girl has been in the delivery room far too long.'

She placed one ear against her Pinard's stethoscope, a special instrument for listening to the internal workings of the abdomen. She could hear the steady, rhythmic beating of the baby's heart but her experienced ear told her that the infant was suffering some distress. The sooner they could deliver the child the better.

Katie held Fatima's hand and wiped her brow, giving her every encouragement as the oxytocin, the intravenous medication, took effect to speed up the contractions. Dr Fielding had positioned himself to take hold of the baby's head as soon as it appeared at the top of the birth canal.

Carefully, he manoeuvred the shoulders into the correct position for expulsion from the mother's body. Katie would have liked to watch the slow descent of the baby but the young mother clung to her hand, obviously unwilling to let her go.

The infant gave a loud wailing cry as Tim Fielding lifted it from between its mother's legs.

'It's a boy!'

Katie saw the delight and amazement in her patient's eyes.

'A son,' the young girl whispered. 'Ahmed will be so pleased.'

For an instant Katie's eyes met Tim's and she smiled happily. She noticed his relieved expression—he'd been as worried as she had, but he hadn't shown it.

The small, extremely competent Night Sister Nasheedha, who'd taken over from Sister Habaid, was giving her full attention to the newborn infant, wiping his nostrils and wrapping him in a sterile towel before handing him to his young mother.

'Thank you, Doctor,' Fatima said, looking up at Katie as she took her newborn son from Sister. 'You have been very kind to me.'

Katie saw the tears of joy in her patient's eyes and felt that it had been worthwhile, intervening. The outcome of the birth might have been the same. On the other hand, she'd seen long, drawn-out, so-called natural births which had resulted in complications. And she hadn't wanted that to happen to this young girl, having her first baby.

She watched Fatima place the baby against her breast
with expert movements that belied the fact she'd never
done this before. She came from a community where,
from an early age, children helped their mothers with
younger siblings. It was a more natural society and many
of the traditions were to be envied by the Western world.

'What a beautiful baby!' she said, as Tim came up
behind her to admire the mother and child, enjoying their
first contact with each other since the birth.

He nodded. 'A precious gift, indeed. Sons are very
important in the family—in any country.'

She smiled as she saw the twinkling in his eyes.
Perhaps he was trying to wind her up again, but she
wasn't going to rise to the bait.

She felt his hand under her arm. 'Come on, we'll leave
our patient to the expert attention of the nursing staff.
I'm going for my run round the island and then I'll take
you into the restaurant for supper.'

He was very sure of himself, this new boss of hers!
Supposing she'd definitely decided to skip supper and
have an early night? It had certainly crossed her mind
as she'd assisted at the birth.

She said goodbye to Fatima and the baby and followed Tim out of the door of the delivery room. Once
again she wondered whether to call it a day and turn in.
Jet lag and the lack of sleep on the plane were beginning
to tell on her.

'I may not be able to stay awake long enough for
supper if I have to wait for you to run round the island
so—'

'Nonsense! It's a very small island and I run very fast.
By the time you've showered and changed I'll be back.
Meet me in the restaurant in half an hour.'

It was an order. Tim high-handed Fielding brooked no

insubordination! She felt like giving him a salute as she swung away from him and hurried over the wooden walkway. She had no idea where he intended to change for his mini-marathon but she was glad he hadn't asked if he could use her bungalow.

In the dim light slanting through the blinds of her bungalow she could see someone moving around. As she reached in her bag for her key the door opened and a smiling house boy in long white trousers and loose, flowing shirt admitted her. On his head was an elaborate blue turban.

'I have just finished,' he told her, with a smile that highlighted the perfect white teeth in his dark face.

The young man slipped out into the warm night, leaving her to admire his handiwork.

The large bed had been turned down and flowers placed on her pillow. In the bathroom fresh towels had been hung and the pile of clothes she'd discarded after the long flight had been removed. She remembered the boy had been carrying a laundry bag. The thought of somebody trawling through her dirty clothes gave her a momentary pang of guilt. Still, if this was the formula for life on Kamafaroo she would happily go along with it!

The water cascaded over her tired body, giving her a new lease of life. As she stepped out of the shower she knew she would be able to survive the evening with her boss. And she was already beginning to look forward to it. He intrigued her already—oh, not in a sexual way; it had been four years since she'd had a flicker of interest in the opposite sex.

The Rat had put paid to that! No, it was his strong personality, his positive attitude, that intrigued her. He was a character; there was no doubt about it.

She flung open the wardrobe doors and surveyed her small repertoire of clothing. The three new floaty dresses that she'd lashed out on for her new life in the tropics were waiting like bridesmaids at a wedding, hoping to be picked to receive the bouquet.

'Now, which of you would like to come out with me tonight?' she said, stretching her still damp arm towards the hangers. 'Eeny, meeny...yes, you'll do nicely.'

Fail-safe cream silk, sleeveless, scooped neckline, but not too low that Tim would get a glimpse of her cleavage and start to get any wild ideas.

That you should be so lucky! said the small voice of reason, and she realised, in spite of her self-protestations, that, yes, she did find him attractive...well, just a teeny bit.

Not dangerously so, thank goodness. The fact that he was a sports freak like the Rat was a definite turn-off. Of one thing she was absolutely certain. She was never going to make a fool of herself again! And she wouldn't allow herself to get into the vulnerable emotional state where any man would have the power to hurt her.

CHAPTER TWO

TIM FIELDING was sitting at a small, round, wooden table on the wide veranda outside the restaurant, overlooking the sea. He stood up as Katie walked across to join him, pulling out a floral-cushioned wicker armchair, into which she sank gratefully, nervously straightening out the cream silk with fingers that had suddenly turned into thumbs.

Her bare legs badly needed a touch of the sun, she noticed as she glanced around the elegant, well-heeled tourists, thronging this obviously popular area of the bar. Most had already dined and were well into the liqueurs and coffee, but a small contingent were still lingering over cocktails before a late dinner.

She noticed that a waiter was hovering behind Tim's chair, his pen poised to take an order.

'What would you like, Dr Mandrake? A cocktail perhaps?' Tim asked, handing her a large illustrated list, which seemed to be self-explanatory in terms of the colours and contents of the exotic cocktails on offer.

She studied the list, very much aware of Tim's eyes upon her. Around her the continuous chatter of the contented tourists mingled with the gentle murmur of the waves rippling onto the shore close by.

There was a Kamafaroo Special, she noticed, apparently containing gin, Cointreau and lime juice, the picture showing a tapered glass with a cherry and a small paper parasol on top. That was certainly an option, but would the gin and Cointreau conspire to make her tired, jet-lagged head go whirling into outer space so that she made a fool of herself in front of her boss?

She glanced down at his glass of tomato juice. That looked fairly innocuous. Best to play safe.

'I'll have one of those, please.'

'Bloody or virgin?' he asked her.

She was completely thrown. 'I'm sorry?'

'This is a Bloody Mary, made up of tomato juice and vodka. If you want it without the vodka they call it a Virgin Mary.'

His expression was po-faced but she sensed he was dying to laugh. Would that be with her or at her? Oh, never mind! She would live dangerously.

'A Bloody Mary,' she said, with the air of somebody to whom cocktails on a tropical island were a way of life.

She took a sip when the waiter had placed it in front of her, resisting the desire to splutter as she smiled across at her companion, whose amused eyes seemed to have been watching her the whole time during this crash course in cocktails.

Don't let him patronise you, said a small guiding voice inside her semi-functioning brain. Start as you mean to go on.

'I'm surprised you drink alcohol if you're following a sports programme,' she said, emboldened by the generous measure of vodka mixed in with the tomato juice.

The dark expressive eyebrows moved upwards again. 'So you're an expert on sports programmes, are you?'

Touché! Get out of that, girl!

'Not really.' She paused, took another sip and decided to come clean. 'I had a boyfriend who was a sports freak. Always rising at dawn to jog around the park.'

He gave her a wide, expansive, knowing grin. 'Hauling himself out of your warm bed—that must have taken some will-power.'

She took another sip of the confidence-inspiring drink. 'Oh, it did.'

Inwardly, she was bristling. This was a blatant attempt to find out whether she and the Rat had shared a bed and it was none of his business.

He ran long, tapering fingers down the side of his sun-tanned cheek, fixing her with a thoughtful look. 'I notice you talked about him in the past tense. Have you come out here to mend a broken heart or—?'

'Certainly not!' She put down her drink and faced him across the table, her brown eyes blazing dangerously.

'I'm sorry.' He leaned forward, looking vaguely contrite. 'I was just making sure that you're going to be emotionally strong enough to handle the work out here. It's not all cocktails in the evening, you know. And if you've arrived with some misplaced idea that this paradise island is going to soothe your jangled nerves, then—'

'I haven't! I'm here to do a job of work. End of story, Dr Fielding.'

Careful, girl, said the inner voice. Not a good idea to antagonise the boss on your first day! Warily, she watched his reaction.

'Do you think you could call me Tim?' he asked in a quiet voice.

Looking across at his wide-set expressive eyes, the confident jut of his darkly stubbled chin, she took a deep breath to calm herself down.

'I might, if you stop asking personal questions.'

'Try it, go on.' He was smiling now, a cajoling sort of smile.

He was trying to get round her, she knew. OK. Bury the hatchet.

'Tim,' she said quietly. 'And...' She paused. 'As we're to work together you can call me Katie.'

She had the impression he was giving a sigh of relief. She really must try not to be so sensitive about her hidden past.

'Is that short for Katherine?'

'No, Caitlin. It's Irish, like my mother.'

'Caitlin.' The name rolled off his tongue. 'That's a beautiful name.'

The expression in his eyes unnerved her. For a split second she thought he fancied her and that would complicate matters. But it would do no harm to get him on her side.

He leaned back in his chair, stretching his long legs underneath the table. One of his canvas deck shoes was almost touching her sandals. Automatically, she curled her feet under her chair.

'Were you born in Ireland, then?'

His voice was brisk and businesslike again, the expressive eyes bland and devoid of emotion. Maybe she'd wanted him to fancy her and had imagined that look he'd given her. Well, he was a very attractive man. It had been a long time since she'd had dinner with a personable, interesting character like this.

'No, I was born in London,' she told him. 'My mother was an aspiring actress who came over to England to go to drama school. She was desperate to become rich and famous.'

'And did she?' The blue eyes flickered with interest.

Katie smiled fondly as she thought about her feisty mother's attempts at fame and fortune.

'No, but it wasn't for want of trying.'

She leaned back against the cushions, looking out across the water at the bright crescent moon, suspended in the midnight-blue darkness which was pierced only by the myriad shimmering stars. She felt mellow with the soothing drink, her mind beginning to function again as the memories flooded back.

'My earliest recollections were of Mum going off to auditions, usually taking me along with her to sit around for hours playing with my dolls or constructing Lego models. She got a couple of parts in some TV commercials, I remember. It was around about the time I was starting school and needing expensive shoes and so on. The money from the commercials helped a lot.'

Tim was a good listener, she decided as she looked at the expressive eyes across the table. He leaned forward, one hand stroking his well-defined chin.

'So your mother never hit the big time?'

She gave him a wry grin. 'We only ever managed to scrape by financially, but it was a fun childhood. Mum couldn't have done more to make it happy for me.'

'And your father? Where does he fit into the picture?'

She hesitated and swirled the contents of her glass, once again feeling uneasy about how to reply. He saw her hesitation and leaned across to put his hand on the side of her chair, his eyes expressively contrite.

'Sorry, that was a personal question. You'd made it clear that your mother was a single parent and I didn't mean to pry. It's the doctor in me, always wanting to get the full case history.'

He leaned back again and she breathed deeply. There was something very exciting about this man. When he'd leaned across just now she'd enjoyed his close proximity. Mmm, what a good thing she'd vowed never to take any man seriously again.

'I don't mind you knowing about my father,' she said quietly. She recrossed her legs under the cream silk.

'There isn't much to tell, really.'

She took a sip of her drink, before placing the glass back on the table and meeting his interested and unnerving gaze.

'My mother had a whirlwind romance with a fellow student when she was at drama school. My father was a bit of a daredevil, apparently. He liked to race his motorbike at unmentionable speeds. One night he was driving through London when a car came out of a side road and ploughed straight into him. The driver of the car survived but my father was killed instantly.'

'I'm so sorry. I wouldn't have—'

'I've accepted it ever since my mother explained what happened,' she hurried on, in the matter-of-fact tone she tried to adopt when explaining what had happened to her father. She'd long ago learned to cope with the sense of loss at never having known him and channelled her feelings into worthwhile activity.

'I was born six months later and Mum was the best mother in the world,' she added.

'Was?' he queried gently.

She smiled. 'Still is, although she's a very bossy character. She was thrilled to bits when I wanted to become a doctor. She told me that she'd always wanted me to have what she called a real profession so that she could boast to her family in Ireland that even if she hadn't got very far up the professional ladder she had a successful daughter.'

She ran a hand over her hair, smoothing back the wayward strands that always congregated in front of her ears.

'But it means Mum wants me to *look* like a doctor.'

He laughed. 'And what is a doctor supposed to look like?'

'Oh, you know, smart clothes and short, well-cut hair and—'

'Don't ever think of having your hair cut off,' he said, leaning across to touch the wisps that had escaped from her chignon. She felt a frisson of excitement, which increased as his fingers brushed her face.

'It's such a pity to trap your hair behind your— Oops, sorry!'

With one dexterous flip of the fingers he had dislodged the crucial couple of grips that had secured her hair. She felt her long brown hair cascading over her shoulders in what her mother would have termed an untidy mess.

He leaned back, his expression that of a naughty schoolboy.

'That's better! You look years younger than…how old did you say you were?'

'I didn't,' she said, trying to look severe but failing miserably.

She mustn't encourage her boss to flirt with her, but on the other hand maybe that was what had been missing from her life for the past four years. Perhaps a little innocent flirtation would put the spark back into her life.

Just so long as it didn't go any further than flirtation!

'Shall we order?' he asked, picking up the menus which had been waiting, unopened, during the minutes when she'd been cajoled into giving Tim a brief outline of her background. The waiter who had placed the menus on the table was still hovering hopefully nearby.

'Can't think why I told you so much about myself just now,' she said, suddenly feeling shy at having revealed details of her life to this relative stranger.

She looked down at the menu in front of her, trying to concentrate.

'I found your story fascinating,' he said quietly, his eyes on the menu. 'It's always interesting to talk to someone who hasn't had a predictable childhood.'

'What do you call a predictable childhood?' she asked, as she ran her eyes down the starters. Mmm, fresh asparagus—that looked tasty.

'The sort that I had,' he said evenly, his eyes still on the menu.

She heard his sharp intake of breath as she listened, fascinated to hear him warm to his subject.

'My father and mother were both doctors in the family firm. My grandmother and grandfather, the founder of the practice, were living nearby to help take care of me when necessary. The whole extended family took holidays in a large farmhouse in Brittany every summer, swimming, boating, fishing.'

He paused and gave a wry smile. 'Oh, don't get me wrong... I was deeply grateful for my secure childhood, but I broke out of the predictable mould as soon as I could.'

She looked up but he was avoiding eye contact. 'How did you break out?'

He gave a short, sharp laugh. 'It's a long story. I don't want to go into it just now. Have you decided what you're going to order, Katie?'

She felt intrigued and disappointed that he wasn't going to divulge more of his past. Maybe when she got to know him better he would open out a bit more.

She closed the menu and put it down on the table. 'I'll have the asparagus followed by the spicy chicken.'

The waiter was scribbling beside her.

'And I'd like the smoked salmon with a fillet steak to follow, medium rare, please.'

They were ushered across to a table at the edge of the thatch-roofed restaurant, looking out through the open sides to the sea. She noticed that there were very few diners still sitting at the tables, and as a result they were served very speedily.

'Your mother sounds a very interesting character,' he said, squeezing a piece of lemon onto his smoked salmon, 'but you haven't told me much about yourself, Katie.'

She spooned melted butter over her asparagus, lifting her eyes briefly to look at him across the table.

'You're fishing again, aren't you, Tim?' There, she'd managed to say his name and make it sound the most natural thing in the world!

He grinned. 'Quite unashamedly wanting to know more about you. Well, we are going to see a lot of each other in the next six months so we might as well get to know as much as we can. I know from your CV that you're twenty-nine and—'

She laughed. 'So you didn't have to ask me just now.'

He pulled a wryly amused face. 'Just checking. You're not married and—'

'Are you?'

She surprised herself at her boldness but this was one question that definitely had to be asked. Not that she cared either way, of course!

A shadow crossed his face. 'No. I got engaged once.'

'And?'

She couldn't believe she was being so persistent! Must be the Bloody Mary, taking her over.

The hint of a frown hovered around his lips.

'That's another story. We're talking about you, this

free-as-the-wind young woman who's come out all alone to paradise island for no apparent reason other than—'

'One reason that I came was to lay the ghost of a relationship that went badly wrong.'

Had she really said that? It had been her voice, right enough, but her lips had seemed to have a life of their own. Perhaps she'd actually wanted to get it off her chest. After all, Tim was already suspicious of her motives, and she could tell he was the enquiring type who wouldn't let up until he'd learned the truth.

'I thought there was more to it than philanthropic interest,' he said quietly.

She was glad that he didn't sound triumphant at having wormed it out of her. That really would have put her off him, and she was enjoying the warm glow of forming a good relationship with the man she was contracted to work with for the next six months.

She looked across at him, warily expecting more questions. How much should she tell him? She really didn't want him to know the unpleasant details about—

'Excuse me, Doctor.' The head waiter was standing beside Tim, his face agitated. 'I'm sorry to interrupt your meal but one of our guests has been taken ill. If you would be kind enough to take a look and give some help.'

Tim was already on his feet. 'I'll get my medical bag,' he said quickly. 'Dr Mandrake will go with you to see the patient,' he called over his shoulder. 'I'll be back in a couple of minutes.'

Katie followed the waiter. In a small space at the entrance to the kitchen she found a young woman sitting on a chair, her face pale with shock, her hand over her mouth. Her distraught companion was beside himself with anxiety as he held his partner's hand.

'I'm Dr Mandrake,' Katie said. 'What happened?'

'Donna was eating some fish,' the young man gabbled semi-coherently. 'Suddenly she started choking. I think—'

'I'd like to take a look down your throat, Donna,' Katie said gently. 'If you could open your mouth wide, I...'

Yes, she could see a large fish bone, lodged at the entrance to the gullet. The young woman must be in considerable discomfort. There wasn't a second to lose because if Donna coughed and dislodged the bone it could disappear from sight and embed itself in tissue that would be difficult to reach without a surgical operation.

'Hold very still, Donna. Please don't move at all,' Katie said, trying to keep the urgency from her voice in an effort to reassure her patient that everything was under control when secretly she knew that every second counted.

Come on, Tim. I need some surgical tweezers instantly! Where was the wretched man? Her patient's colour was deteriorating; she was turning blue and—

'Improvise in an emergency,' her surgical professor had always said. His voice from the past materialised inside her head.

'Open my handbag,' she told Donna's companion in a confident tone that belied the butterflies in her stomach. 'In the central compartment with the lipstick you'll find some eyebrow tweezers. Pass them to me, please.'

The young man's hands were shaking but, amazingly, he located the tweezers in two seconds flat.

What a good thing she'd tidied out her bag, before travelling out here, she thought as she took the tweezers between her thumb and index finger.

Donna made a slight gurgling noise at the back of her throat, closing her terrified eyes as Katie bent over her.

She had only one chance to get hold of this bone. Deftly she closed the tweezers around it, neatly whipping it out of the soft tissue at the back of the throat.

'There!' Relief swept over Katie as, triumphantly, she held up the bone to show that the delicate operation had been successful.

Tim arrived behind her, obviously out of breath, and looked down at their patient.

'What's the problem?'

'It's OK,' she told him in a confident, matter-of-fact voice. 'A fish bone lodged in the throat. I've removed it. Donna was very brave and co-operative.'

The young woman looked up at Katie. 'Thanks ever so much, Doctor. I was so glad when you turned up like that. My gran swallowed a fish bone once and she had to go into hospital.'

Katie nodded. 'Well, that was what I was trying to avoid.'

'Mind if I take a look?' Tim said. 'I'm sure Dr Mandrake has made a perfect job of this.'

Donna opened her mouth wide again. Tim shone a torch around the back of the throat.

'Absolutely perfect! A slight tear where the bone implanted itself but that will soon heal on its own. It certainly won't spoil your holiday.'

'Actually, we're on honeymoon here for a couple of weeks,' the young man said. 'Just arrived today. I think jet lag was getting to Donna and she didn't concentrate enough. I love the fresh fish you get out here, straight from the sea, but you've got to be careful with the bones.'

'Well, go and enjoy the rest of your honeymoon,' Tim

said. 'You can pop in to see Dr Mandrake any morning at the little hospital through the palm tree grove if you need any more help. She holds a surgery there from nine to eleven.'

There were more profuse thanks from the young couple before Tim and Katie were able to resume their places at their table.

'That was quick thinking on your part, Katie,' Tim said, his eyes watching her reaction to his praise.

She was pleased to note the admiring expression in his eyes as he looked at her across the table. Nothing like getting in the boss's good books at the beginning of her contract.

'I wanted to pull it out before it slipped any further down. I didn't fancy having to set up the operating theatre at this hour of the night.'

She put her hand over her mouth to suppress a yawn. 'I'm beginning to think I'll have to get off to my bed soon,' she admitted quietly.

He shook his head. 'Not before you've eaten your spicy chicken.'

She looked down at the plate which the waiter had just placed in front of her. Yes, it looked and smelled delicious. She would keep her eyes open long enough to eat this.

The waiter reached into the ice bucket at the side of the table and poured her another glass of cold white wine. She opened her mouth to protest but then decided it wouldn't make much difference. She would sleep it off before morning. And it was a particularly excellent wine.

'No dessert, just coffee,' she said, as she put down her knife and fork.

Coffee would keep her awake long enough to finish

her evening with Tim. He was still looking bright-eyed and bushy-tailed, she noticed, even after a hard day in the operating theatre at the Indira Gandhi Hospital in Male. Still, he hadn't been awake for…how many hours was it now? She'd lost count.

She looked across the table at Tim and found her eyes were playing tricks with her. For a moment she'd imagined it was Rick. She opened her eyes wide. Tim was nothing like Rick, well, except in outline. Wide, muscular shoulders, long, sinewy arms—

'Am I under scrutiny for some reason or…?'

'Sorry!' she said, realising that she'd been staring at him.

'I'm having difficulty staying awake, and for a moment you looked like someone else. But you're absolutely nothing like him, really,' she tailed off, feeling embarrassed that she'd ever started to explain.

He smiled and leaned back in his chair, the languorous almost animal-like movement once again reminding her uncomfortably of the man who'd double-crossed her.

'Are you trying to tell me I reminded you of your ex-boyfriend?' he asked, his voice suddenly husky.

She took a deep breath. 'Only in so far as you're sitting across a table from me and you're a man, an athletic-looking man who, in a dim light, ignoring the hair colouring—'

'Oh, come on, Katie, spit it out. Let's put a name to this unknown character. I'm all intrigued.'

Tim was leaning forward now, a boyish expression of excitement on his face. She decided there was no earthly reason why she shouldn't tell Tim her ex-fiancé's name. He couldn't possibly have heard of him, and she was here to lay the ghost after all. Talking about the Rat and what a dreadful man he was might be therapeutic.

She gave a wry smile. 'My mother called him the Rat after he made off with my savings and spent them on another woman. The name kind of stuck after that.'

'Sounds a most appropriate name for him. But his real name is...?'

'Rick Baldwin,' she said quietly.

She saw a startled expression cross Tim's face and she assured herself that it wasn't remotely possible that he'd heard of Rick.

'And you say he's athletic?' Tim asked in a matter-of-fact tone.

'Very. As far as I know, he's a sports master some-where in the north of England. He came down to London when he was between jobs, and that was when I first met him.'

She sucked air through her clenched teeth as she re-membered Rick's two-faced onslaught on her affections.

'Charm simply oozes out of him and I was completely swept off my feet, as they say in all the romantic stories. We had six months together during which he persuaded me to open a joint bank account with him in preparation for our wedding and the honeymoon of a lifetime.'

'He's not by any chance a diver, is he?'

Katie frowned. 'Well, yes, that's one of the sports he's good at. In fact, before our honeymoon that never hap-pened he told me he wanted to teach me to dive when we came out...' Her voice trailed away as she saw the worried expression on his face. 'Tim, do you know something that I don't?' she asked nervously.

He put his hand across the table and took hold of hers. She felt reassured by the pressure of his fingers, but she waited with bated breath until he spoke again.

'There's a Rick Baldwin who's a diving instructor on the nearby island of Fanassi. I don't suppose—'

'No!'

She removed her hand and clapped it to her face. 'It couldn't be Rick. As I told you, when he came out here four years ago with that...that woman...he was only planning to stay for a couple of weeks. He was due to start this well-paid job in a sports college afterwards. The plan had been that he would then be able to pay back all the money he owed me, but I never heard anything about him after—'

'Well, I hope for your sake it's not the same man. I've met Rick Baldwin a few times. We've actually dived together. He seems an interesting character, very charming and...'

He stopped and their eyes met across the table.

'Very charming,' Katie repeated in a deadpan voice as she felt her pulses beginning to race. 'Yes, Rick can be very charming when it suits him—if there's something to be gained by it. But I can't see how he could possibly be out here still.'

She ran a hand through the mass of hair falling over her shoulders. 'No! It must be somebody else with the same name. I refuse to believe that...'

'I've only been working out here myself for a few months. I heard that this Rick Baldwin had been here for a couple of years. It's possible that after his illicit holiday, courtesy of your savings, he went back to his job in the UK and then took up this diving appointment later on.'

She swallowed hard. 'What does he look like, this diving instructor?'

'Oh, tall, broad-shouldered, longish fair hair—' He broke off as he saw her obvious dismay.

She shivered as she heard the description of fair hair. Oh, God! Could this nightmare really be happening?

Could the Rat really have spirited himself out here to haunt her?

'I'll make enquiries if you like,' Tim finished off.

'No, no, don't! If it's the Rat I'll just make a point of avoiding him.'

'But you said he owed you money.'

'Hah! I wrote that off a long time ago. I couldn't bear the thought of having to make contact with him.'

'Have you any idea why he left you like that?' Tim asked gently.

She leaned back and closed her eyes as the memories flooded back. 'He'd started complaining that I never had time for him, that I was always working.'

'And was this true?'

'Of course it was true!' She attempted to adjust the high-pitched decibels in her voice.

'Sorry, I didn't mean to be rude,' she continued in a calmer voice. 'But you know what it's like when you're doing your year as a junior house-surgeon. I was working all the hours that were sent and he was swanning around, staying in bed—in my flat—until lunchtime and then expecting me to have the energy to go out on the town at night.'

He pursed his lips. 'I'm surprised you didn't kick him out.'

She gave him a wry, self-deprecating grin. 'With the benefit of hindsight, so am I! But it was the first time I'd become besotted with a man and it was like being under a spell. Believe me, I'll never allow myself to get in that condition again!'

'I know how you feel!'

She stared across at him as she heard the vehemence in his voice.

'Don't tell me the same sort of thing happened to you!'

He gave her a sardonic smile. 'You mean falling for the wrong person?'

She watched as he frowned. But it was a fleeting frown. A mere fraction of a second elapsed before he smiled again and resumed talking in a relaxed way.

'Oh, yes, it happened to me all right, but I reckon she did me a good service because I've had some wonderfully enriching relationships, without the hassle of being tied up. It's surprising how many people there are in the world who prefer to stay uncommitted.'

She nodded, feeling an emotion akin to relief yet, unbelievably, tinged with disappointment. 'Yes, there are a lot of us about.'

His smile broadened. 'But what would you do if someone tried to cast his wicked spell over you again?'

With an impatient gesture she reached back with both hands, tossing her hair from her shoulders until it settled behind her ears and flowed down between her shoulder blades, skimming the triangle of white skin at the top of her dress.

'I wouldn't let it happen! Romantic love isn't for me any more. I'm a clear-headed, hard-working professional woman and I can live without it. I mean, who needs it?' she finished off defiantly, trying to convince both of them of the validity of the advice she'd been giving herself ever since Rick had absconded.

'Well said! I only hope you can live up to your resolutions.'

'Oh, I certainly will!'

The effort involved in her pronouncement had induced some more jet lag and rendered her exhausted. She stifled another yawn with the back of her hand.

'I really must go and get some sleep. Did I overhear you say I have to take surgery at nine tomorrow?'

Glancing at her watch, she saw it was after midnight. 'I mean today.'

He leaned towards her, the expression in his eyes sympathetic. 'Theoretically, but I'm not a slave-driver. You've had a very long day and a half since leaving London and I'm staying here on the island tonight. I'll take the surgery for you. Go and have a good sleep and meet me at the hospital at midday.'

She breathed a sigh of relief. She was warming to this new boss. 'Thanks a lot.'

She stood up. He came round the table, looking down at her with a continuing expression of sympathetic concern in his eyes which she found very touching.

'Will you be able to find the way back to your bungalow?'

'Of course!'

She didn't want him to think she was some helpless female who needed escorting to her door even though she did feel as if she was in the middle of a sleep-walking dream.

She pointed out through the open sides of the restaurant. 'It's straight along that path and—'

'No, it's that way,' he said, laughing as he pointed in the other direction.

He put his hand under her elbow and steered her towards the door. 'Jet lag is making you disorientated. You'll be OK after a good night's sleep.'

The touch of his fingers on her arm was unnerving her more than her jet lag as she walked beside him along the sandy path. They crossed the wooden walkway to her bungalow. All around her the lapping of the sea mingled with the clicking sounds of the insects.

She fished the keys out of her bag. Tim reached forward, took them from her and put them in the door, before stepping back as the door opened.

'Goodnight, Katie.'

'Goodnight, Tim.'

There was a brief, awkward moment as she looked up at him and felt the sudden desire, in spite of her jet lag, to invite him in for a nightcap. But she resisted the temptation. One, he might turn her down and, two, she didn't want him to get the idea she was making advances.

Which was the last thing in the world she planned to do—wasn't it?

CHAPTER THREE

IT MUST have been the unfamiliar sound of the waves that had woken Katie. For a few seconds she thought she was listening to the traffic outside her London flat. Then she noticed the fan, whirring around in the ceiling above her, and she registered that she was on Kamafaroo in her water bungalow.

At some point in the night she remembered getting up to switch off the intrusive droning of the air conditioning, changing to the gentle humming of the fan which had been infinitely more soothing. Although she'd been completely exhausted before she'd got into bed, for some unknown reason her mind had suddenly sprung into action, reviewing the events of the evening with relentless detail.

Tim, her new boss, had been a central figure in her fight for sleep. His face had recurred over and over again, sometimes superimposed on the hated features of the Rat. It had all been terribly confusing and she was delighted to find that she'd actually managed to sleep for a few hours.

Glancing at her watch, she saw it had been more than a few hours. Heavens above! She was due at the hospital in half an hour.

Leaping out of bed, she ran into the shower room. She emerged a few minutes later with her wet hair draped over her shoulders. She spent five minutes with the hair-dryer and two minutes throwing on a clean cotton dress and flat, open sandals, before racing out across the wooden walkway.

A shoal of multicoloured fish, swimming leisurely underneath her, seemed to epitomise her new way of life on this paradise island. She really must try to be calmer and more relaxed in this tropical climate if she hoped to keep healthy.

The midday heat hit her when she emerged from the artificial coolness of her bungalow. By the time she'd negotiated the path through the palm trees and reached the hospital she was beginning to feel the dampening of her skin. Her semi-dry hair lay coiled in her nape, adding to the general feeling of humidity.

The same pretty nurse, her long, dark plait snaking down her back, was sitting at the desk in the reception area of the hospital.

She smiled at Katie. Was it her imagination or did Nurse Sabia seem more friendly this morning? Perhaps word had got round that Katie was actually keen to do some medical work and wasn't just someone looking for a good time on a holiday island.

'Dr Fielding is waiting for you in Outpatients, Dr Mandrake,' the nurse told her. 'I will show you the way.'

Katie smiled. 'That's OK, Nurse Sabia. I know where it is.'

She found Tim with a young boy from the village, stitching up a wound in his leg.

'Good morning, Doctor,' he said, lifting his eyes momentarily from the patient. 'Or should I say good afternoon?'

She hoped this wasn't a veiled criticism. After all, it had been Tim who'd suggested she slept late this morning.

'Depends whether you've had lunch or not,' she said evenly, 'and I haven't even had breakfast.'

He held up his hands in mock horror. 'Go and get something to eat. Can't have you fainting away on me.'

He reached for his scissors and snipped the final suture.

'There you go, Musa, you're as good as new. Come and see us again in a week's time and don't fall out of any more trees in the meantime.'

The dark-skinned boy grinned, displaying dazzling white teeth, as Tim helped him down from the couch. The boy's shy young mother peeped out from her all-encompassing white cotton head covering and took hold of her son's hand.

'Thank you, Doctor,' she said, in a hesitant, barely audible voice.

Tim smiled encouragingly. 'This is Dr Mandrake, who's going to be looking after you for a few months,' Tim said. 'She'll usually be here in the mornings, and the hospital will know where to find her in the afternoons and evenings.'

'Sounds like I'm on twenty-four-hour call,' Katie said with a wry smile as mother and son went out.

'That's what it sounds like, but actually you should have plenty of free time. You just have to be available when...'

His voice trailed away as Sister Habaid burst into the cubicle, waving her arms anxiously to convey that she wanted to interrupt their conversation.

Tim put his scissors into a kidney dish and whipped off his surgical gloves. 'Yes, what can I do for you, Sister?'

Sister Habaid clenched her hands together. 'A diving

accident, Doctor, over on Fanassi. The instructor has radioed for immediate help.'

'I'm on my way. Katie, you'd better come with me. The morning surgery is finished and there's nothing Sister and her staff can't handle here without us.'

A feeling of nervous apprehension swept over her as she reviewed Sister Habaid's information. The instructor on Fanassi had radioed for help. What if this instructor really was...?

'Come on, Katie!'

Tim's brusque voice interrupted her thoughts, galvanising her into action. She couldn't shirk her duty if Tim had requested her to go with him.

In a matter of minutes they had boarded the speedboat, waiting for them down by the jetty, and were hurtling across the narrow strip of water that separated them from the island of Fanassi, carving a white-foamed swathe through the dark blue sea.

Through the open door she could see an inner cabin with bunks around each side. The outer cabin, open at the back, had padded seats, but she and Tim had elected to sit on the wooden bench at the stern to take advantage of the fresh air. The three-man crew who were manoeuvring the boat were up on the top above the outer cabin.

Glancing up the metal ladder towards the three small figures, she thought they looked very young to be in charge of a powerful boat like this, but she comforted herself with the reflection that they'd probably been working on boats, helping their fathers and grandfathers, since they were children. Perhaps only on fishing boats, but they must have graduated to powerboats because of their extreme competence—she hoped!

Due to the speed of the boat there was a cooling

breeze on her face which she found very refreshing. It was helping her to think clearly about what she was going to do if this diving instructor actually was Rick.

'These diving accidents can be very tricky,' Tim said, his expression grim. 'If it's serious I'll have to airlift the patient or patients to the hospital in Male.'

'Did you say the island we're going to is called Fanassi?' Katie asked nervously.

Even in the midst of the emergency she had registered that Fanassi was the island Tim had mentioned last night where this man called Rick Baldwin was an instructor. Was she going to come face to face with the Rat or would it turn out to be someone else and she'd be spared the ordeal?

'Yes, I said it was Fanassi,' Tim said evenly in a firm voice that reminded her she would have to shoulder her responsibilities whatever happened. 'This may be embarrassing for you if Rick Baldwin turns out to be—'

'Tim, don't worry about it,' she said quickly, her eyes scanning the water as the coastline of Fanassi island came ever nearer. 'I'm here to do a job of work. If this Rick does turn out to be the Rat, I'll simply ignore him and get on with helping you with the patient.'

'And talking of doing a job of work, you ought to eat something,' he told her, reaching into a box under his seat marked EMERGENCY SUPPLIES.

He handed her a sealed packet of oatcakes and a bottle of mineral water.

'Breakfast,' he said solemnly.

Somehow her appetite had subsided. 'I'm not sure if I could manage—'

'Eat!' he told her, as he tore open the packet and held a biscuit towards her mouth. 'And keep drinking lots of water as well.'

She gave him a mock salute as she crunched her teeth into the surprisingly tasty biscuit. 'Yes, sir!'

He smiled. 'I'm not being totally altruistic. Unless I keep you in good health I'll have to do your work as well as my own.'

Katie smiled back, noticing the way his mouth crinkled upwards at the corners. Always a good sign. The Rat's lips had been usually in a set line and bent downwards when he couldn't get his own way. Oh, he'd smiled a lot in the early days, but towards the end of their ill-fated partnership he'd been surly and morose.

What on earth had she seen in him in the first place? Why hadn't she, quite literally, smelled a rat when his behaviour had changed? She deliberately banished the questions which had so often occupied her since Rick disappeared.

A spray of salty water flew up over the side of the boat and splashed across her face. Peeping over the side, she could see a myriad multicoloured fish, seemingly trying to keep pace with the boat. The water was deep but transparently clear. She could see a coral reef way below them. And then, suddenly, a huge turtle swam into view.

Relieved to have something to take her mind off the relentlessly approaching shoreline, she turned to point out the turtle to Tim, but by the time he'd leaned over the side it had vanished into the depths.

'The sea around these islands is a constant source of fascination,' Tim said quietly. 'It can be great fun, exploring the depths, but it can also be very dangerous…sometimes fatal,' he finished, grimly. 'That's why nobody cuts corners in the standard of diving. Our instructors have to be first class.'

She saw that he was watching her carefully, his

thoughts obviously on Rick Baldwin. She drew in her breath. In a matter of minutes she would know the worst.

'Tim, if this sports instructor is the Rat,' she said slowly, enunciating carefully so that she could be heard over the sound of the engines, 'it won't make any difference to the way I cope with the medical emergency. I can be professionally detached when the occasion demands.'

He put out his hand and touched her bare arm, causing her to give an involuntary shiver as she realised that she wasn't immune to the feel of a man's fingers.

'I'm sure you can, Katie.'

She swallowed hard as she looked into his emotionally charged eyes. Here was a man you could depend on...couldn't you? Would she ever be able to learn to trust again? Tim was certainly good at his job but what was he like as a man? Looking the way he did, wouldn't he turn out to be cast in the same mould as—?

Stop it! she told herself as she put the odious comparison out of her mind. Why she was even thinking about it she couldn't imagine.

They were reaching the shore. A group of young Maldivian men were waiting to help their crew tie up the boat at the wooden jetty.

One of the onshore men, in a white cotton T-shirt and shorts, signalled to Katie and Tim that they were to follow him to the diving school.

Katie could feel her pulses racing as she stepped inside the long, low, wooden building, set back from the beach in a glade of palm trees. At the side of the diving school she could see several wetsuits, hanging up to dry, on the covered veranda that encircled the building. Air tanks were lined up like small soldiers on sentry duty, guarding the door.

The first thing she noticed when she followed Tim inside was the patient, lying on a couch, his torso covered with a white sheet. Blood was seeping through the portion covering his legs. An oxygen mask covered the lower part of his pallid face, while his wet brown hair dampened the pillow.

A tall, fair-haired man, in white T-shirt and shorts, with his back to the door, was leaning over him. He turned at the sound of their footsteps.

'Thank goodness you're here, Doctor. I...' His voice trailed away as he stared at Katie.

She covered her hand with her mouth to stop the involuntary cry that threatened to escape from her suddenly dry mouth. She moistened her lips. Her worst fears had now been confirmed.

'Tell me what happened, Rick,' Tim said quickly, taking the seemingly shell-shocked instructor on one side, as if realising that he himself was the only one in control of his emotions at that moment. 'Katie, check the oxygen flow to the patient.'

She was on automatic pilot as she swung into action. With her head down and her eyes on the patient as she critically examined and assessed his condition, she adjusted the flow, before placing her stethoscope on the man's chest and listening to the irregular rhythm of his heartbeat.

She was a doctor, first and foremost. She was here to save this patient's life. Nothing else mattered. That man over there with the long fair hair who was talking to Tim was merely a diving instructor and had nothing to do with her.

She registered snatches of Rick's explanation. Something about Jim, their patient, staying down too long in an undersea cave and then coming up too quickly. His buddy—that was the name for a diving partner, she remembered from the handbook she'd read on the subject—Sue had returned slowly to the surface and had suffered no ill-effects, apart from a couple of cuts caused by the sharp coral.

Katie glanced across at the frightened young woman, sitting beside the prone figure of her buddy. Her teeth were chattering in spite of the high early afternoon temperature—definitely in a state of shock.

'I was running out of air so I got myself back to the surface very slowly, but Jim came up too quickly, Doctor,' she said, her moist eyes wide with fear. 'He's going to be all right, isn't he? He hasn't got the bends, has he?'

Tim came up behind her and leaned across to examine their patient. Katie waited for him to answer the frightened young woman's question.

'We're going to take Jim over to the hospital in Male,' Tim said gently, folding up his stethoscope. 'We'll put him in the decompression chamber and that should alleviate the symptoms of the bends.'

The young woman wiped a tissue over her eyes. 'What exactly happens when divers get the bends, Doctor?'

Tim put a hand on the back of her chair, his eyes expressively sympathetic as he explained.

'If a diver comes up too quickly from the different atmosphere deep down in the sea, nitrogen bubbles can form in the bloodstream, causing decompression sickness.'

'Will he—?'

'Now, don't worry,' he hurried on. 'I'm not saying this has happened to Jim, but we're going to play safe and put him in the decompression chamber in hospital for a couple of hours or so.'

Katie picked up a blanket and draped it around the young woman's shaking shoulders, being careful to avoid the cut on her upper arm. Someone had attempted to stem the flow of blood with a cotton bandage but it looked as if it would require further attention. She'd better check it out.

In the background she could hear the diving instructor, telephoning for the air ambulance. She still refused to think of him as anything other than the man in charge of this diving centre. All her defence mechanisms were instructing her to pretend she'd never met him before in her life.

She cut through the soggy cotton bandage to reveal the extent of Sue's injury. Hmm, that was going to require a few stitches and the sooner the better.

Tim was totally involved with the other patient, fixing up a saline drip, so she delved into her medical bag for a sterile suture pack. Gently she explained to Sue what she intended to do and wiped the skin with a local anaesthetic, before inserting the stitches. Finally, she sprayed the whole area with an antiseptic, plastic-forming spray cover.

'Thanks, Doctor,' Sue said quietly. 'I've got another cut on my leg where I got caught up in some coral. It's a bit painful.'

Katie found that the leg injury was more extensive than the arm wound. She handed her patient a couple of strong painkillers and a glass of water.

Tim touched her arm. 'The helicopter's here. I'm going to take Jim over to Male. I'll deal with his cuts and lacerations over there. Sue can stay here and rest on the island after you've sutured that leg wound. No point dragging her all the way over to the hospital. We're short of beds so she'll be more comfortable in her own bungalow.'

'Fine!' Katie said, her voice quavering as she realised she was going to be left behind in Rick Baldwin's diving centre.

She'd assumed she would have made a quick escape over the sea with Tim. But he was quite right. Sue looked as if she needed rest so that she could recover from her ordeal.

'I'll call you on Kamafaroo this evening,' Tim was saying, as he helped to load Jim on to a stretcher.

'Yes. I'd like an update on our patient,' she said, in what she'd intended to be a professional tone but had actually come out in a breathless rush that sounded as if she'd been running a marathon.

Taking a deep breath to steady her nerves, she fixed her eyes on Sue's leg wound and reached down to swab the skin with local anaesthetic.

She paused in mid-suture as she heard the roar of the helicopter, the whirring of the blades becoming less audible as it made its way over the sea. She wished fervently that she could have gone with Tim. He would have been such a help to her while she came to terms with her shock at meeting up with Rick.

Hey, steady on! Whatever was coming over her? She'd only known Tim a few hours and already she was becoming to rely on him being with her.

She reached for her surgical scissors. Get a grip on yourself, girl! Got to keep your independent spirit.

She realised, with a pang of horror, that she was alone with the Rat. But you've got a patient, a few staff and some hangers-on, she reminded herself quickly in an effort to boost her confidence.

Bending her head over the wound, she gave all her powers of concentration to the patient.

'How does it feel, Sue?'

'I can't feel the stitches going in and I'm not looking at it. That cool liquid you put on made my leg nice and numb.'

'Good. I'll soon be finished and then you can go and have a rest in your bungalow.'

The room seemed very quiet. Perhaps the Rat had gone—or was he skulking around in a corner, as rats did?

'There you go, Sue!' She smiled at her patient as she snipped the end off the suture. 'All done. You'll be good as new when that heals.'

'Thanks a lot, Doctor. When do you think Jim will come back from hospital?'

'I'm afraid I couldn't say at this stage,' Katie answered diplomatically. 'I'll ask Dr Fielding to give you a call this evening after he's phoned me.'

'Thanks. Jim isn't my boyfriend, you know,' Sue said quickly, a slight pink flush diffusing her pallid face. 'We only met last week when we were paired up as buddies for the diving course. But he's been a good friend and I feel very concerned about him.'

Katie smiled as she patted her patient's hand. 'Of course you do.'

'You see, I can't help thinking it was my fault. You're supposed to stay together when you're buddies, but because I'd been breathing too deeply and had used up my air supply the instructor had to take me back to the surface. Poor old Jim was left on his own in the cave and I think he may have panicked and—'

'You mustn't blame yourself, Sue,' Katie said gently. 'Jim made the decision to surface quickly. Dr Fielding will get him into the decompression chamber and do everything he can to make him well again. I'll phone you this evening when I've had a report from him.'

'Thanks a lot, Doctor.'

'The name's Katie, and don't worry.'

Sue gave a rueful smile. 'I'll try not to.'

Katie turned and gave a swift intake of breath as she saw that Rick was leaning against the nearby wall, watching her. His eyes didn't flinch as she looked straight at him.

'Do you have a wheelchair?' she asked tersely.

'Of course, Doctor.'

He was biting his lower lip, a habit she remembered from way back, usually signifying that he was nervous. And his hooded green eyes had retreated into slits as he scrutinised her.

'Then perhaps you could escort Sue back to her bungalow. I'd rather she didn't have to walk for the next few hours.'

She kept her voice deliberately cool and professional. This man was beneath contempt and not worth wasting her emotions on. As soon as he'd set off with Sue she would beat a hasty retreat to the speedboat, and in a few minutes she would be safely back on Kamafaroo.

With extreme calm Rick walked to the door and leaned out to snap his fingers at two young men, sitting on the wooden veranda.

'My assistants will take Sue,' he said evenly. 'They are one hundred per cent reliable. We need to talk, Katie.'

'I don't think we have anything to say to each other,' she snapped.

She turned away to supervise the two young men who were preparing the wheelchair.

'Oh, but I think we do,' he said in a loud voice.

Her shell-shocked mind registered his emotionally charged tone as she tucked the blanket around Sue's shoulders, handing her sports bag to one of the assistants.

'Take it easy, Sue. Try and get some sleep.'

The young woman flicked her long blonde hair out of her eyes with her uninjured arm.

'Thanks, Katie, I will. Don't forget to call me, will you?'

Katie smiled reassuringly. 'Of course I'll call you. But sleep first.'

Turning from the doorway, she realised that she was really alone with Rick now. His broad, muscular back was towards her as he bent over the fridge in the corner of the room. She noticed for the first time the posters fixed to the back wall, illustrating different kinds of fish. She tried to concentrate on the beauty of the fish in an effort to rid herself of the angry feelings which were like a physical pain inside her head.

She knew that if she gave vent to her feelings of revulsion towards this man it would be like a nuclear explosion! She had to stay calm. Nothing would be achieved by—

'Drink?' He held out a can of beer towards her.

'No, thanks. I've got to get back. I've got patients to see and—'

He gave an exasperated sigh. 'Sister Habaid has been running Kamafaroo hospital on her own for years. Another few minutes isn't going to make any difference.'

She ignored him as she began to walk down the veranda steps.

'Why have you followed me out here if you don't want to discuss what happened?'

She stopped dead in her tracks and turned, her eyes blazing.

'Don't flatter yourself, Rick! Do you honestly think I'd come halfway round the world to see you? I would cross to the other side of the road if you were walking towards me!'

She clenched her hands as she reminded herself not to lose her cool. Nothing would be achieved by indulging in a slanging match.

'For your information,' she continued in a quieter tone, 'this is just one of those unhappy coincidences that life sometimes throws at you.' She turned back to the path, her footsteps even more determined.

'It wasn't what you thought, Katie,' he called after her, standing on the top step, his body poised as if to run after her.

She hesitated, intrigued to know what kind of excuse he could possibly dredge up.

She half turned towards him. 'Wasn't it?'

'I had my reasons for leaving like that.'

'Did you?' She clasped her hands together to stop herself from trembling. 'And your reasons were…?'

He ran a hand through his fair hair, which fell around his ears almost to chin level. She noticed that he looked tanned and fit. There was no doubt that he would be having a whale of a time, pulling the birds on a paradise island like this. The unsuspecting tourists would swoon into his arms because he was a very handsome-looking man with his athletic build. Pity the dark side of his character didn't show until you got to know him!

He raised the can to his lips and took a long drink.

Wiping his mouth with the back of his hand, he gave her a long, slow smile.

'My reasons were very complicated. I don't intend to explain myself here in the heat of the afternoon sun. One evening I'll take you over to Male and—'

She turned on her heel and marched off down the path towards the jetty.

'In your dreams!' she called over her shoulder.

'Katie, just give me a chance to explain!'

That was more like it—a hint of a grovel!

The crew of the Kamafaroo speedboat were already revving up the engine as she approached, one of them holding out his hand to help her aboard. She stepped in and sat in the stern, her eyes firmly set on the distant coastline of Kamafaroo.

She would make a point of trying to avoid any more contact with Rick. He'd pulled the wool over her eyes and swindled her—that was all there was to it. The only good thing to come out of her relationship with Rick was that in the four intervening years she'd become a much tougher character. Thanks to that disastrous experience, she'd lost her naïve, trusting nature and become much more worldly-wise.

The boat hurtled forward, and she started to enjoy the feel of the hot sun on her upturned face and the droplets of spray, cooling her skin. Little by little she found she was regaining her sense of equilibrium. With any luck she wouldn't have to meet up with Rick again. She would make a valiant effort to forget his existence, just as she had done for the last four years.

Suddenly, out of the depths of the sea, close to the boat, a shoal of dolphins began what looked like a deliberate marine show, displaying their leaping athleticism for her benefit.

'Oh, look! How beautiful!' She stood up and leaned over the side.

The crew, up the ladder above her, who had probably seen dolphins cavorting many times, waved down at her, seemingly pleased by her enthusiasm as she watched the dolphins leaping in wide arcs from the water.

As the boat outstripped the dolphins' display she sat down again. The happy interlude had helped to dispel the ravaging effects of her enmity towards Rick.

Mmm, life was good when you maintained your independence!

And tonight Tim would be phoning her. Only to give an update on our patient, she reminded herself. Still, it would be nice to hear his voice. She already felt he was a real friend. Someone she could trust.

They were approaching the shore. She gathered her medical bag and shoulder-bag beside her on the seat. She felt as if she was coming home, which was a good sign that she was settling in.

After a couple of hours in the hospital Katie went back to her bungalow, ate a couple of bananas, promised herself she'd eat a proper meal that evening, stretched out on the bed and closed her eyes.

It seemed only minutes later that the phone interrupted her sleep.

'Katie?'

'Oh, hello, Tim.'

She felt a surge of excitement as she struggled to sit up on her bed. She'd meant to have five minutes' rest but she must have been asleep for ages.

Through the slatted blinds she could see that the sky was dark already.

She cradled the phone against her ear as she took a

sip of mineral water from the bottle at the side of her bed to lubricate her dry mouth. 'How's Jim?'

'Still in the decompression chamber. He's responding to treatment but we'll have to be very careful with him.'

She heard the rustling of papers at the other end.

'Where are you, Tim?'

'Still in hospital. I've got a mass of paperwork and later on I've got a Caesarean section.'

She felt her spirits drop. Half of her had been hoping he might have come over that evening, but she told herself she was being unrealistic. Just because she'd made friends with the boss didn't mean they had to spend their off-duty time together. It would be a good thing if she put a limit on that sort of thing in case she got too involved.

She heard more paper rustling and then Tim asked, 'How's Sue?'

'The wounds should heal quickly. She's a healthy young woman. I told her to rest for the afternoon. In fact, I've promised to call her to let her know about Jim.'

'Yes, I think you can tell her he's going to make a full recovery.'

'Good!' She hesitated, wanting the phone conversation to continue and search around for something to say. 'Jim isn't Sue's boyfriend, you know.'

It sounded a rather lame remark, even to her own ears! Would he see through her attempts to keep him talking?

And why, exactly, she asked herself, was she trying to prolong this phone call? Wouldn't it be advisable to keep their relationship on a strictly professional level?

'Yes, I know—they were paired up as buddies, weren't they? Still, Sue will be pleased to know Jim's going to be OK. How did you get on with Rick after I left?'

Katie gave a derisive snort. 'He wanted to discuss what happened four years ago but I refused to listen to his fabricated excuses. He actually had the gall to suggest he take me out one evening and explain. I mean, what is there to explain? I can guess all I want to know about the sordid situation where—'

'Katie, calm down! I know you've been badly hurt but don't you think it would help to find out if Rick had any kind of mitigating circumstances for his actions?'

She took a deep breath. 'You sound like a lawyer for the defence. What possible excuse can he have for absconding with my savings?'

'I think you should try to find out. If you don't it will only stay at the back of your mind and you'll never get rid of the feeling that you've been wronged. If it's any help I'll come with you if you decide to meet him. A third, uninvolved person would help to keep the meeting on an even keel.'

She was caught unawares. The idea was certainly worth considering.

'You'd be willing to do that?' Her voice had risen to a plaintive squeak.

'Katie, I'm in charge of the welfare of all my staff.'

She thought she detected a hint of exasperation in his tone as he began to explain further.

'I have an obligation to make sure they stay healthy, and that includes seeing to it that they have peace of mind. If you've been traumatised by this man then the matter has to be resolved, and the sooner the better.'

She hesitated. When he'd first shown interest in her involvement with Rick she'd thought it had been on a more personal level. Correction—she'd *hoped* he'd been involved on a more personal level! Now, having heard his professional explanation, she discovered that half of her was relieved and the other half disappointed to hear that he merely regarded her as one of his staff.

She was simply an obligation for him. If she didn't try to resolve her problem with Rick then Tim might come to the conclusion that she wasn't in a fit state to hold down her job.

She drew in her breath. 'OK, I'll set up a meeting with Rick at some point in the near future—so long as you'll be available to act as referee. Rick can be very difficult to handle.'

'Don't worry, I'm used to handling difficult people.'

He paused, and she could hear his light, rhythmic breathing over the phone. She could picture him somewhere out there across that great expanse of moonlit sea, sitting in his office with the fan whirring above his head—or did he prefer air conditioning?

'And, Katie...'

She heard a softer tone in his voice.

'Yes?'

She held her breath as she waited, hoping, in spite of herself, that he was going to talk on a more personal level.

'I definitely think you're taking the right course of action. You can't leave this problem, hanging over your head indefinitely. Hasn't Rick ever tried to contact you in the past four years?'

'No!'

Her deep-down, pent-up anger with Rick helped to mask the frustration she felt that Tim had become completely professional again.

'That's one of the questions we'll have to put to him—the reason why he simply disappeared.'

His tone was abrupt, terse almost. There was more

paper-shuffling and then Tim said, 'Look, I'll have to go now. Anything to report from the hospital?'

'It's been a routine sort of afternoon. Sister Habaid has everything under control. Fatima's husband, Ahmed, came in to admire their baby son. He wanted to take Fatima home but I persuaded him to leave her with us for a few days. She needs to build up her strength—don't you agree?'

'Of course, but she'll have plenty of help from her family, especially her mother and grandmother. We shouldn't try to change their way of life. I'll see if I can find the time to come across and see her tomorrow.'

Her spirits had lifted at the prospect of seeing him again but drooped immediately as he said he had to go.

'Goodnight, Katie.'

'Goodnight.'

She broke the connection and dialled Sue's number on Fanassi. A few minutes' conversation, assuring her patient that Jim was well on the way to recovery, brought her back to her senses. Sue assured Katie that she was feeling comfortable and had been pampered with room service.

However, as soon as Katie put the phone down and eased out of her professional concern her thoughts went back to Tim.

What, she asked herself as she walked out onto her wooden veranda poised above the sea, was happening to her? Why did she feel all goose-pimply when the temperature out here was still in the eighties?

She sank onto one of the cane chairs, her eyes scanning the moonlit surf. On the far horizon she could see the string of bright lights that was Male, shining like a glittering necklace on the dark, mysterious, velvet cloth of the sea.

He was over there and she was over here. What a waste when they could be together!

She gave herself a ticking-off. This was how it had all started with Rick. Imagining she needed to be with him. Convincing herself that life was better when she was in a twosome. She'd only known Tim a matter of hours and she was already fantasising about him.

Since Rick had deceived her so badly she hadn't felt the slightest desire to form a relationship with another man. Quite the opposite! She'd actively discouraged any advances. She seemed to have lost the ability to feel deeply.

But Tim was different.

A warm, gentle, sea breeze blew across her face, ruffling her hair. She ran a hand over it, remembering how Tim had told her she mustn't cut it. So he had taken an interest in her as a woman, hadn't he?

She didn't want a real relationship with him. She didn't want to get involved. Just a little touch of romance and she would be satisfied. Not even an affair. Especially not an affair with all the entanglement of commitment!

No, this time she would know when to stop. She would hold the reins and keep her head.

Hey, steady on! You don't even know how Tim feels about you. He's been scrupulously correct. You don't even know if he's free to indulge in a little light-hearted romance.

No, but she intended to find out!

CHAPTER FOUR

LYING back on her bed with one hand under her neck, staring up at the whirring fan as it attempted to cool the afternoon heat, Katie reflected that she'd been on Kamafaroo a whole month and had still not been over to explore Male, the capital city of the Maldives. She would especially like to look around the hospital where Tim worked most days.

She'd actually hinted as much to Tim on his last visit to Kamafaroo but he hadn't taken her up on it. He'd said he would arrange a visit during a quiet period when he wasn't so busy, but the promised visit hadn't materialised yet. Maybe she should take the matter into her own hands. After all, no one could object to a member of the medical staff simply turning up at the hospital in Male—could they?

She took a sip from the water bottle on her bedside cabinet while she gave the matter some thought. Here she was on a beautiful tropical island with two whole days off duty. The duty roster Tim had given her had stated that she could take off one whole day a week, at her own discretion, when the workload allowed it.

Last week she'd been kept very busy with a group of resident tourists who'd seemed particularly accident-prone. In spite of warnings not to touch the coral, when snorkelling and swimming, several of the tourists, underwater cameras at the ready, had somehow managed to cut themselves in their enthusiasm to swim after the attention-grabbing, all-enthralling fish.

Just when she'd thought she might be able to take a couple of hours off she'd been called out again to suture a wound and prescribe the relevant antibiotic.

And, worryingly, a large number of the tourists had succumbed to a diarrhoea problem which had meant she'd had to keep them in the hospital or visit them in their bungalows during the forty-eight hours when they'd been at their worst. This had been the worst outbreak of its kind for some time, so Sister Habaid had told her, but it seemed to have died down since that particular group of tourists left the island.

Had the outbreak continued, she'd intended to make a thorough investigation of their eating, drinking and hygiene habits to try to pinpoint what had been causing it. But the problem had resolved itself, thank goodness!

This week had been quiet so far, and Sister Habaid had insisted that Katie took two days off to compensate for the extra time she'd put in last week.

She smiled as she swung her legs off the side of the bed. Sister Habaid had finally thawed out during the time they'd worked together and they now had mutual respect for each other.

She'd explained to Katie, in one of her rare moments of confidentiality, that she hadn't seen the need for a resident doctor on Fanassi. Patients had always been transferred to Male when necessary, but Sister had come to the conclusion that it was, indeed, more convenient to have a qualified doctor on hand—if only to speed up the facility for getting prescriptions, she'd added, probably to make sure that Katie didn't overestimate her importance!

As Katie padded across on bare feet to the bathroom she reflected that she was glad she'd got one of the relationships sorted out.

Her relationship with Tim, however, was very much on ice. She'd only seen him on brief occasions when he'd flown in to check on a patient and had flown straight back to Male. He'd been courteous and professional, but the warmth she'd thought she'd sensed on that first day had been lacking.

She turned on the shower and stood underneath it, allowing the spray to bounce off her warm skin. As she cooled down she told herself she must have imagined Tim's interest in her. It had been purely professional—nothing more, nothing less.

Just as well! Because she wasn't sure how easy she would have found it to remain uninvolved with someone like Tim. She'd never felt such strong attraction to anyone before and it would have been difficult not to get carried away by the surge of emotion she'd felt. Especially after the arid desert of the last four years!

Emotional involvement was one thing she had to guard against if she were ever to find herself in the midst of a light-hearted romance. It should be possible, but with a man like Tim—

The shrilling of the phone interrupted her thoughts. Wrapping a towel around herself, she returned to her bedroom and stretched out on the bed as she answered it.

'Tim!' Too late, she realised that her voice had been too welcoming for a junior colleague, greeting her boss.

Fortunately, he seemed to misinterpret her tone. 'Don't worry, I know it's your day off so I'm not going to ask you to work. It's a personal call.'

She swallowed hard. This was more like it! 'How can I help?'

'I spent a couple of hours diving on Fanassi early this morning. I like to keep up my diving when I get the chance. It was a good thing I was there because there was a minor incident with one of the new students. I brought him back here to the hospital and put him in the decompression chamber for an hour. It was only a precaution and he's OK now. A bit shaken but nothing serious.'

He paused and she held her breath for a few seconds, before saying, 'I'm glad it's nothing serious.' Then she hesitated but simply had to ask, 'I suppose you saw Rick?'

'Yes, he came down with us.' A long pause. 'He wants to see you, Katie.'

'Why?' She couldn't help snapping at him.

'Hey, steady on! Don't shoot the messenger.'

'I'm sorry,' she said, in a mollified tone. 'But if you think I'm—'

'He says he needs to talk to you. Are you free this evening?'

'I don't want to see him on my own, Tim,' she said firmly.

Wild horses couldn't have dragged her to confront Rick on a one-to-one basis.

'Of course not. I promised to be the third person, remember?'

She took a deep breath. The matter had to be resolved now that she'd seen Rick again. It had been relatively easy to blank him out of her consciousness when she was working in England but here in the Maldives the situation was difficult. Knowing that any day she might have to meet him in a professional situation had increased her apprehension.

'OK, where?'

'Meet me here at the Indira Gandhi hospital about six. I'll give you a brief tour and then we'll go back to my apartment. I'll phone Rick and tell him to meet us there about eight.'

'I'm glad that I'm finally going to be shown our main hospital. As for the meeting with Rick...' She hesitated, rolling on to her side and taking the phone in her other hand. 'I'm grateful to you for setting this up, Tim, but...I'll be glad when it's over.'

'Don't worry, Katie. I'll be there for you.'

'Thanks.'

She put the phone down, remembering the gentle tone he'd adopted at the end of their conversation. Was he like this with all his staff?

Probably! said the inner voice of sanity. Stop fantasising about him!

What should she wear this evening? Surveying the contents of her wardrobe, she chose cream linen trousers and a black silk shirt. Even though the shirt had long sleeves, the silk would help to keep her cool during the confrontation with Rick.

She was relieved to find that Tim was waiting for her in the lobby of the hospital. Well, not exactly waiting so much as carrying on an intense conversation with a couple of medical colleagues, but he did break off and smile as she approached.

'Dr Afraz, this is Dr Mandrake.'

She was introduced to a tall, rather intense-looking, dark-skinned young man who held out his hand, grasping hers in a firm handshake before hurrying away, pleading pressure of work.

'Dr Afraz takes over my patients on occasions,' Tim explained. 'I've got to go to a medical conference in the near future so we've had a meeting together today. And this is Dr Bandira. Dr Mandrake is working on Kamafaroo for a few months.'

The slim, young Indian doctor extended a hand from the folds of her colourful sari.

'I'm happy to meet you, Dr Mandrake. How do you find working conditions here in the Maldives?'

'Hot!' Katie said, smoothing down the linen of her trousers and wishing she'd worn a skirt. Something cool and swirling like Dr Bandira's sari would have been much more comfortable in the sweltering heat.

'But in spite of the heat, I'm enjoying my work here,' she hurried on, not wishing to appear churlish.

'I'm pleased to hear that,' Dr Bandira said. 'Now, if you'll excuse me, I must go home to my family.'

Katie watched the diminutive figure, walking elegantly towards the main entrance, while Tim explained that Dr Bandira was a consultant paediatrician. 'She also has a husband and three children so she's a very busy lady.'

'She obviously manages to juggle family and career successfully,' Katie said, feeling the familiar pang of something akin to envy.

She felt Tim's hand under her arm, steering her away down the corridor.

'It can't be easy, but Dr Bandira is a very capable woman,' he told her.

'Obviously.'

'Do I detect a wistful tone?'

'Good heavens, no! I wouldn't want all that commitment. Life is difficult enough being a career girl without having to rush home and cook the supper.'

That was what she'd been advocating for the past four years and usually she managed to convince herself. But at this moment, with Tim's hand under her elbow, it wasn't easy to pretend she'd totally renounced the idea of love and marriage. She knew, deep down, that if the right person came along, someone she could really trust...

'Let's have a cooling drink before we start the tour of the hospital.'

He was opening a door, stepping aside so that she could walk into what was obviously his consulting room. A large desk dominated the end of the room; two chairs were set on the side where the patients would arrive. She sat down on one chair and watched Tim open a small fridge and take out a glass jug.

'Freshly squeezed orange juice.' He handed her an ice-cold glass. 'I drink masses of the stuff out here. I'm probably overdosing on vitamin C but it means I stay healthy.'

He sat down, his long, outstretched legs almost touching her sandals. She noticed with dismay the chipped nail varnish on her toes. How did anybody manage to juggle husband, children and exacting job and still look as elegant as Dr Bandira when she herself couldn't even cope with basic grooming?

She would never be able to cope with such a lifestyle so it was as well she'd decided to stay single, wasn't it? Her career was all-important to her. But a little light romance wouldn't go amiss—

'Penny for them!'

He was smiling at her with an intrigued expression.

'Oh!' She put a hand to her face as she felt a flush spreading over her cheeks. 'I was lamenting the fact that I should have redone my toenails. When I was walking barefoot beside the sea this morning the sand scraped and scratched them and—'

'Only superficial scratches,' he said solemnly, bending down to take one of her feet in his large, capable hands.

'Do you think I'll live, Doctor?' she asked, adopting a light-hearted tone.

Nobody had ever taken her foot in their hand like this before. At least, not since childhood when her mother had ticked off each toe as they'd played at 'this little piggy went to market'. The memory made her smile and helped to keep in check the tingling feeling in her foot that Tim's grasp was arousing.

Gently he removed her sandals. 'You'll be much cooler when we set off again.'

He was kicking off his own shoes. 'I always go bare-foot whenever I can in this part of the world.'

She saw that his bare toes were now only inches from hers on the polished wooden floor. The feeling of intimacy between them was reaching alarming proportions...at least for her! It didn't seem to be affecting Tim.

'When you're recovered enough I'll take you round the hospital. But for the moment just relax.'

She loved the way he pronounced the word 'relax'. Sort of soothing...promising more? Now, don't get carried away, she chided herself quickly as she looked across into the depths of those expressive blue eyes and felt a shiver of excitement. Mirrored in his eyes she thought she detected a glimmer of interest.

He leaned forward and touched the tip of her nose.

'Fascinating!' he said, his lips forming a deliciously sensual smile. 'Your little turned-up nose suits your face exactly.'

So it was to be a light flirtation. Great! She could handle that.

'I should hope so! It's the only one I've got and it's been there a long time.'

Oh, this was going to be fun! Nothing heavy or serious. Mmm, she certainly could relax and enjoy herself with a man like this.

He laughed, a sensuous, sexy sound that sent an involuntary shiver down her spine. 'Twenty-nine years isn't a long time. You're only a youngster.'

'I suppose, from your advanced age of...?'

She gave a deliberately provocative smile as she paused, waiting for Tim to supply a number.

'Thirty-nine,' he said, giving her a rakish grin.

'Ah! Older than I thought.'

Her tongue was running away with her. She was talking for the sake of talking, saying the first thing that came into her head—anything to sustain the exciting rapport that she sensed building up between them.

Her cheeks felt flushed. Had someone switched off the air conditioning? She smoothed her damp palms down the sides of her linen trousers as she opened up the conversation again.

'As I was saying, from your advanced age, you probably feel qualified to dispense advice on the secrets of life and—'

'The secrets of life?'

His tone was suddenly cautious. She hadn't meant to change the frivolous nature of the conversation but it was too late now. Tim's easy expression was now much too serious.

He leaned back in his chair and ran a hand through his dark hair, chasing the strands that had escaped over his forehead.

'If only! To be honest, I've come to the conclusion it doesn't matter how old you are—life is still full of surprises. Still full of situations that are difficult to cope with.'

From the earnestness of his tone, she could tell he was speaking from the heart. He'd lived life to the full, this man, and lurking beneath that capable, worldly-wise veneer was a very vulnerable soul. A soul that had been hurt, perhaps? He'd hinted as much on their first night in the restaurant.

'Who was she?' Her lips had formed these words quite independently. She knew she had no right to pry, remembering how she hated it when others tried to prise her secrets from her. But she had to know. It was important to understand this man before...before what?

What was her subconscious self planning in spite of all her resolutions? Only a light-hearted romance, her sensible self reminded her. Nothing serious.

She watched him putting the tips of his fingers together, studying them as if those experienced, talented, surgeon's hands might hold a clue as to what this life was all about.

'Who was who?' he asked, in a remarkably calm voice, considering she was being far too curious.

'Your disastrous relationship woman.'

He raised his eyes to hers and she saw the hurt in his expression.

He hesitated, before speaking in a slow, deliberate voice, as if making a confession. 'Her name was Rebecca.'

'Nice name.'

It was a trite remark but she hoped to stimulate him into making more revelations. She waited, but he was merely frowning, still studying the tips of his fingers. Then all at once he began to talk again, the pain evident from the expression on his face.

'I first met Rebecca when she was a sister on the same cruise ship. All my medical knowledge tells me there is no such fever but, believe me, when I first saw her I was struck down immediately by that incomprehensible condition known as love at first sight.'

'Not another sufferer!'

He gave a harsh laugh. 'You were afflicted, too, I remember. It's a severe complaint. Fortunately, it's not terminal.'

He stood up and moved over to the window, tipping the struts of the blinds so that he could look out at the gathering darkness.

'We ought to get a move on if I'm to show you round the hospital,' he said briskly.

She felt a profound sense of disappointment. 'But aren't you going to tell me any more about Rebecca?'

He swung round, a look of astonishment on his face. 'Good heavens, no! I've never told anyone about my relationship with Rebecca.'

'Maybe you should,' she said gently. 'It sometimes helps to talk.'

For a split second he seemed to be wavering but obviously thought better of it.

'Perhaps it might,' he said in a barely audible tone, almost as if he'd forgotten she was there. Then, raising his voice, he said very firmly that it was time for him to show her round the hospital.

She pulled on her sandals, fastening the buckles with fingers that seemed all thumbs, and stood up. He was waiting for her beside the door, an enigmatic smile on his face. Gently he reached down and tilted her chin so that she had to look up into his expressive eyes.

'Maybe one day I'll tell you some more about

Rebecca,' he said, his voice husky. 'We've both got ghosts to lay, haven't we?'

She blinked as she saw the tenderness in his eyes. He was lowering his head and for one breathtaking moment she thought he was going to kiss her. She felt her eyelids flicker and almost closed them in delicious anticipation.

Thank God she kept her cool because he was straightening again, obviously coming to his senses! It would have been so embarrassing if she'd been blatantly waiting for the touch of his lips. The thought of those full, sensuous lips only inches from her face was inducing some wickedly pleasant feelings deep down inside her.

'Ready?' He was holding open the door.

She nodded. She was ready all right but not for a tour of the hospital! With a valiant effort she forced herself to concentrate on what Tim was telling her as they walked together down the white-walled corridor.

'This is a very modern, well-equipped hospital. We can handle difficult and advanced surgery here. This is the operating theatre suite.'

They turned in through swing doors. A team of white-uniformed nursing staff was engaged in clearing up after the surgical operations of the day. One theatre was in use, a red light above the door indicating that they weren't to enter.

Katie was introduced to the nursing staff. Tim knew each one by name and it was obvious from their wide, friendly smiles and deferential manner that they found him easy to work with, while at the same time holding him in high esteem.

'This is only a whistle-stop tour,' he whispered as he put a hand under her elbow and guided her out through the swing doors back into the corridor. 'We can't spend

much time in each department if we're to make our eight
o'clock appointment.'

She groaned. 'I hope you realise I'm dreading this
meeting.'

'You've got to face up to it,' he said firmly.

They were entering an orthopaedic ward. The sight of
so many bedridden patients, their limbs immobilised
with traction and pulleys, made her see how unimportant
her own problem was. At least she was physically fit and
all in one piece!

Tim was right to encourage her to have this meeting
with Rick. She had to find out what had really happened
and resolve her enmity towards Rick one way or another
before her life could move on to the next stage. After
all, that was why she'd come out to the Maldives wasn't
it?

After the orthopaedic ward Tim gave her a brief round
of one of the surgical wards followed by the paediatric
unit, where it was difficult to escape from the adorable
children who were convalescing and wanted them to stay
on and play.

Finally, they visited the obstetrics unit. One mother
whose baby son was only hours old told Tim she was
having difficulty with feeding. Katie offered to help the
mother with her infant, while Tim went off to see a new
antenatal patient whom the obstetrics sister had requested him to examine.

Katie smiled to herself as she thought that nobody
seemed to be taking into account that they were tech-
nically off duty, but she didn't mind. It was impossible
to say no when a patient needed help.

Sitting on the side of the young mother's bed, Katie
cradled the little newborn boy in her arms while the
mother settled herself comfortably back against the pil-

lows. The mother held out her arms to show that she was ready and Katie placed the baby against his mother's breast.

The baby lay motionless, his tiny mouth firmly shut. A big tear escaped the mother's dark brown eyes. Quickly glancing at the patient's chart, Katie learned that her name was Masoodha. This was a mother who was going to need some tender loving care.

Guiding her patient's hands and speaking very quietly, Katie showed Masoodha how to hold the baby's head against her breast, whilst gently stimulating his little rosebud mouth with her finger. After a short time the baby gave a tiny spluttering noise at the back of his throat and Masoodha held him away from her in alarm.

'It's all right, Masoodha,' Katie said, gently repositioning the baby. 'Your little son is opening his mouth now. See, he's hungry. He's trying to take your nipple in his mouth and...'

She gave a sigh of relief as the baby's lips encircled the mother's teat. Even out here in the Maldives, where childbirth was a much more natural event, some mothers still needed the encouragement and confidence that she'd had to give them in the UK. Basically, maternity care was the same the world over.

There was an air of new-found confidence showing in the way the mother was smiling now.

'Thank you, Doctor,' she said shyly.

'He's a lovely baby.'

Katie looked wistfully at the short, silky, dark hair, the little hand placed so trustingly on his mother's breast as he sucked noisily.

She clenched her hands in her lap as she reflected that it was such a pity you had to make a real commitment before you could embark on motherhood. During the last year she'd sometimes wondered about the possibility of becoming a single mother but she'd discarded the idea as not being remotely viable. Children needed two parents.

For a few months, with her thirtieth birthday looming on Valentine's Day—only a couple of weeks now—she'd found herself dwelling on her biological clock. She was in her most fertile years, as her hormones kept reminding her! Was she going to ignore her fertility during these vital years, simply immersing herself in her career until her hormones stopped nagging her?

A rustling of the cubicle curtains made her look up. Tim was standing behind her. 'You seem to have sorted out the problem here,' he said quietly.

She smiled up at him. She'd solved the patient's problem but would she ever solve her own?

'How was your antenatal patient?' she asked quickly, trying to assume a professional manner.

'I've advised Sister to let the labour take its natural course. In view of the size of the foetus and the small bone structure of the mother, Sister was wondering whether a Caesarean would be necessary. I've done an extensive examination and I'm convinced it's not.'

'That's good news.'

Katie stood up, her hair brushing against Tim's chin as he simultaneously leaned forward to check on the feeding baby.

They both laughed at the painless collision and the tenderness in his eyes made her catch her breath. Hurriedly, she reminded herself that his tender expression was for the benefit of the baby—wasn't it?

'We'd better get a move on,' he said, glancing at his watch.

'Don't want to keep the Rat waiting,' Katie said, under her breath.

They said their goodbyes to the young mother, who was now leaning back in a relaxed manner, as if she'd been feeding babies for years.

'You'd better stop calling him the Rat,' Tim said wryly, as he handed Katie a glass of orange juice. 'Give the poor chap a chance to explain himself.'

She took a sip of the juice. Tim had told her he'd made the ice cubes with bottled water so they were perfectly safe. She swirled the contents of the clinking glass and allowed the pleasantly cold drink to soothe her. Got to keep cool. She glanced at her watch. Ten past eight. Trust Rick to be late!

She put her glass on the nearby table. 'You're sure he'll come?'

'You know him better than I do.'

She picked up her glass again. She'd inadvertently placed it on one of Tim's medical journals and the condensation had made a wet ring. She took a tissue from her bag and began nervously dabbing.

Tim's hand closed over hers. 'Leave it, Katie,' he said gently. 'It doesn't matter. It will dry soon enough. Get yourself composed and think what you want to ask Rick.'

He removed his fingers and she raised the glass to her mouth to take a large gulp.

'What don't I want to ask?' she said vehemently.

He gave her a wry smile. 'Sure you still want me to mediate?'

'Oh, please, don't leave me!'

It had been an involuntary cry from the heart and she felt embarrassed, but Tim didn't seem to mind. She watched him as he leaned back in his cane armchair, his long chino-clad legs stretched out in front of him. His bare, sun-tanned feet were tapping a silent tune on the coconut matting that covered his wooden floor.

He looked totally at ease in this little haven of calm he'd created across the courtyard at the back of the hospital. There were several other doctors living in this small, purpose-built building but Katie was sure that none of the apartments would be as interesting as this one.

In some ways this living room resembled a marine museum! There were three large pictures of multicoloured tropical fish on the walls; books on diving and yachting magazines mingled with the medical journals on the two small coffee-tables. Tim's wetsuit hung in the corner of the room by the large window that looked out over the hospital grounds.

Through one of the doors leading from this room was a small kitchen. That was where Tim had disappeared and made fridge-opening noises when he'd got their drinks. And the other closed door was probably Tim's bedroom. Best not to think about what went on in there...the adoring girls who would flock to be with him to soothe his fevered brow at the end of a long day and—

There was someone knocking on the door, mercifully interrupting her unwelcome flight of fancy.

'Are you ready for this?' Tim was standing by the door, his hand on the handle.

What a question! It was too late now to back down. She nodded. 'Let's get it over with. You'd think at least he could have made it on time.'

'Hi!' Rick strode into the room and sank into the chair that Tim had been occupying. 'I arrived at half past seven but you weren't here so I've been to see Jim, our diving casualty, up on the medical ward. He seems fine now, doesn't he?'

Well, at least she couldn't accuse Rick of being late! She resolved to try and give him a fair hearing. She noticed that he'd made an effort to look smart—clean, well-pressed jeans and cotton shirt, his long fair hair neatly imprisoned at his nape in a thin, black band.

'Drink?' Tim asked, crossing the room towards the kitchen.

'Thanks, I'll have a beer.'

As long as it was only one, Katie thought, remembering how belligerent Rick became when he'd been drinking. She'd got to get her answers before the beer started addling his brain.

Tim put the can of beer and a glass on the table nearest to Rick, before settling himself on a high-backed chair beside Katie. She felt safer now that Tim was only inches away. She could reach out and touch him for reassurance.

Rick ignored the glass and raised the can to his lips. 'Cheers!' He took a deep draught, then put down the can and wiped his mouth with the back of his hand. 'Now, where shall we start?'

Tim leaned forward, an earnest expression on his face. 'As I see it, you've got some explaining to do, Rick. Why did you leave Katie and go off with another woman, taking the contents of your joint account?'

Rick's narrow green eyes flickered. 'Is that what Katie told you?'

'Do you deny it?' Tim asked evenly.

Rick hesitated before a frown spread over his thin-lipped mouth. 'No, but hear me out. Don't rush me.'

Tim leaned back. 'Take all the time you need.'

Rick took another swig from his can. 'I don't suppose either of you know what it's like to be brought up in care.'

'I don't suppose you do either,' Katie put in quickly. 'You were born with a silver spoon in your mouth so if you're going to invent some sob story for Tim's benefit forget it.'

Rick stood up, beer can in hand, and walked over to the window where he stood for a few seconds with his back towards them. When he turned round he was staring directly at Katie.

'I wasn't, as you put it, born with a silver spoon in my mouth,' he said quietly. 'I told you that story about my father coming from a wealthy family in Scotland to impress you. I never knew who my father was and my mother put me in care when I was a baby.'

Katie turned to look at Tim, who was thoughtfully stroking his chin. This unexpected revelation had left her temporarily speechless. She remembered the elaborate details Rick had told her about his grandfather's Scottish castle.

'Rick, you told lies to Katie about your background initially so why should we believe this new story?' Tim asked slowly.

Rick was biting his bottom lip. 'Look, I'm really sorry I misled her. You've got to believe me—I'm telling you the truth. I was brought up in a children's home, then fostered and then dumped back in the home again. I was determined that when I grew up I'd get a decent life for myself.'

'And this decent life meant telling a few lies along the way, did it?' Katie asked. 'Why couldn't you have told me the truth when we first met? It wouldn't have made a scrap of difference to—'

'Yes, but I wasn't to know that!'

Rick crossed the room and sat down again. 'I'd been turned down before by classy birds like you. This time I was determined to be accepted.'

'And you were,' Katie said quietly, 'so why did you spoil it by—?'

'I was heavily in debt before I met you. I suppose you could say I'd been living beyond my means when I was at physical education college. But I had a goal to achieve. I was good at swimming and after I'd joined the college diving club I knew that was what I wanted to make a career of. All I needed was some money to pay off my debts and get me started.'

'So you decided to take my savings,' she said in a flat, resigned tone.

'It wasn't like that, Katie. I was truly fond of you. I wanted us to be together but you never had time for me.'

'I had my career to work on! I was on the bottom rung of the ladder, the hospital dogsbody, always available for emergencies. My social life was low on my list of priorities.'

He took a step forward, a concerned expression on his face.

'I know, and that's why I decided I had to get out of your life so that you could get on with your career. I didn't want to leave but I could see I was holding you back and...'

He put down the beer can, leaned forward and put his head in his hands. For one awful moment Katie thought he was going to start sobbing.

'I did it for you, Katie,' he said, in a barely audible voice.

He was either a very good actor or... She drew in her breath, perplexed by Rick's uncharacteristic display of emotion. What was she to make of him? In the six months he'd lived with her she'd never seen him like this.

'And the little matter of the joint savings account and the girl who shared it with you?' Tim put in dryly.

Rick sucked air in between his teeth as he clenched his jaw.

'I met Carol in a pub when Katie was working one of those long duty sessions at the hospital. She was married, older than me but with a very healthy bank account. Her husband kept a mistress and couldn't care less what Carol was up to. I think she was lonely. She suggested we went on holiday together and I steered her towards the Maldives. I wanted to find out if I could get a job here.'

Katie gave a deep sigh. 'So you took our money and—'

'I knew Carol would pay for the holiday but I needed to pay off my plastic card bill and keep something to live on after she'd gone back to England. I couldn't get a job here but I stayed on for a few weeks until the money ran out. I left a job application form at the diving school and asked them to contact me when they had a vacancy. Then I went back to the north of England and worked in a sports shop.'

Katie frowned. 'I thought you had a job lined up in a sports college. You were planning to work there while you applied for jobs nearer London.'

Rick shook his head. 'I don't know why I told you that.'

'Probably to impress,' Tim said wryly. 'I'm not sure what to believe but—'

'You've got to believe that I'm sorry all this happened. Ever since I got this brilliant job in charge of my own diving school on Fanassi I've been trying to save up so I could pay Katie the money I owe her.'

'Trying to save up?' Tim queried. 'How successful have you been?'

'Well, you know, even with all the responsibility of my work, I don't get much of a salary, but I manage to put a little bit by each month and—'

'And you were planning to contact me and send me your debts, were you?' Katie said.

'Of course!' Rick said, his eyes wide with injured pride as if she had no business querying him.

'So why didn't you contact me before?'

'I did! I called the flat but you weren't there and the answerphone wasn't working. When I finally tracked you down at your mother's she called me a rat and put the phone down on me. And then when you didn't answer my letter I—'

'What letter?' Katie gave an exasperated sigh.

'I've got to hand it to you, Rick—you can tell a good story!' Tim said. He stood up and walked over towards Rick, scrutinising him carefully.

'You know, Rick, I think your problem is that you have difficulty separating fact from fiction. But you're extremely good at your job. I've seen you in action with your diving students and you've obviously found your niche in life. I've never heard one word said against you out here. Otherwise, I would have been advising Katie to take legal proceedings.'

'But I've told you I'm going to pay her back! That was always my intention. However else I've let you down, I'm not a thief.'

Katie watched in amazement as Rick pulled a cheque book from his back pocket and started scribbling furiously. He signed his name with a flourish and handed over the cheque.

'One hundred dollars,' Katie read, with a feeling of unreality.

'We'll work out the balance and let you know how much more you owe,' Tim said evenly.

'You'll have to be patient,' Rick said. 'As I've said—'

'Don't worry, we're not going to lean on you. I'll get my solicitor to—'

'No solicitors, please!' Rick said quickly. 'I want this kept on a friendly basis, just between the three of us.'

Katie looked at Tim to see if he agreed. Slowly he nodded.

'OK. I'd like us to remain friends. You run the best diving school around here and I don't want to have to avoid going over there when I want to spend some of my off-duty time diving.'

Rick smiled. 'Thanks.'

He held out his hand and the two men shook hands. Turning to Katie, Rick said, 'I'd like to be friends with you, too, Katie. Why don't you come along with Tim for a course of diving lessons?'

She gave an involuntary shiver. 'No, thanks.'

Her thoughts were in turmoil. Tim and Rick had shaken hands, but had her problem really been resolved? There were questions still unanswered. Had he really phoned? Had he actually written to her? Or was it all a pack of lies? As Tim had pointed out, Rick had difficulty separating fact from fiction.

'Another drink?' Tim was standing up, reaching for Rick's empty can and her empty glass.

'I'd like another beer,' Rick said.

Katie stood up. 'Not for me. My boat crew will be wanting to get back to Kamafaroo.'

'I could drop you off when—' Rick began, but she cut in with a polite refusal. The thought of speeding across the dark sea with Rick was too much for her.

Tim put down the empties and came towards her. 'Sure you have to go? I was going to make supper. I cook a brilliant omelette and my salad with French dressing is—'

'Another time, perhaps.'

As she moved towards the door she realised she was still dazed by Rick's revelations. She wanted to go back to the sanctuary of her own bungalow to think things over. Rick looked settled for a long drinking session and she didn't want to stay in the same room with him to watch him getting slowly more obnoxious.

Tim opened the door, took her arm and guided her out into the corridor. Firmly, he closed the door behind them. She looked up at him and saw the concerned expression in his expressive blue eyes.

'Are you OK, Katie? I'd prefer you to stay. We need to talk, to discuss what Rick's told us. I'd hoped this meeting would have helped you but—'

'It has,' she tried to assure him, but her voice faltered. 'I'm tired. When I've had time to think it over I'll feel better.'

'I want to help you all I can, Katie,' he said, his voice soothingly calm.

And then he kissed her.

She had no warning that it was going to happen. He simply took her face between his hands and placed his lips against hers in a long, tenderly caressing kiss. She closed her eyes to savour the moment, wondering if she were in the middle of a dream.

He moved his hands away from her face and took her

in his arms, holding her so firmly against his broad, muscular chest that she could feel the beating of his heart.

How long they stood like this she had no idea. Gently, oh, so gently, he released her, but not before she knew that he must have been aware of the sensual desires he'd roused in her.

'If you insist on going, I can't stop you,' he whispered huskily. 'But you don't have to go. I could get rid of Rick and you could stay.'

Did he mean stay as in stay the night or stay for another drink? She hesitated, her heart pounding, one half of her aroused to a sensual fever pitch, the other telling her to back off before it was too late. This could be the first step towards some kind of commitment. Was she sure she was ready for this?

'I could put a radio call through to your boat crew,' he said, a tantalising smile playing on his lips.

She drew in her breath as she made a split-second decision.

'I must go.' She was trying desperately to convince herself that she was doing the right thing. She was playing safe so she would have nothing to regret when the sensual heat died down.

'Goodnight, Tim.'

CHAPTER FIVE

KATIE switched off the alarm clock and swung her legs over the side of the bed. Reaching towards the controls on the bedhead, she turned up the air conditioning. The weather was definitely getting hotter. It was difficult to believe it was February and, according to the two-day-old newspaper she'd managed to get hold of yesterday from an incoming tourist, there was snow in the UK!

She took a long drink of water from the bottle on her bedside table as she reflected that it was a couple of weeks since she'd seen Tim. She'd spoken to him on the phone a few times but only in connection with their work. He'd been pleasantly friendly but there had been nothing in his manner to suggest that he remembered having taken her in his arms with such tenderness that it took her breath away even to think about it.

Was he regretting it? Did he think he'd upset her, by coming on too strong? After all, she'd been the one who'd turned down the offer of a cosy night together.

If that had been what Tim had really been planning. On the other hand, was it possible that she'd read more into it than he'd meant?

Why had she turned him down like that? She realised now that it had been because she'd just been reminded of the emotional wounds that Rick had inflicted when he'd double-crossed her. The feeling that she could never trust a man again—any man—had been revived. And the commitment involved in abandoning herself to a night of sensual, light-hearted pleasure had been too much for her.

But now, two weeks afterwards, the scars were beginning to heal again. Was she able to put the past behind her? Maybe she could with a man like Tim.

Katie wrapped a sari around her in case the house boy came into her room while she was in the shower. Most of the time it was more comfortable to wear nothing at all when she was alone in her bungalow with the blinds closed.

She turned the shower to cold but it came out warmly tepid. She needed to keep cool today if she was to tackle the disturbing problem of this new outbreak of diarrhoea among the tourists. She stepped out of the shower and flung a towel around her.

She would have to phone Tim. She'd mentioned the problem when the first patients had come to see her at morning surgery five days ago, and he'd asked her to keep him informed. The tour company was also sending faxes, exhorting her to find out why Kamafaroo, with its previously unblemished health record, had suddenly developed this medical problem.

Katie dabbed herself dry, wrapped the sari around her again and went back to the bedside phone. She swallowed hard. Got to stay professional. Got to forget the feel of Tim's arms around her. Making a conscious effort, she dialled his direct line. With any luck she should catch him before he left his room.

'Tim, it's Katie.'

'Good morning, Katie.' His voice was still muffled with sleep.

'Did I waken you?'

'Mmm, but don't worry. I need to get moving. I had a late night.'

She heard the rustle of sheets and imagined him lying there naked, or with a single sheet wrapped around his long, muscular, sun-tanned legs. A late night, he'd said. Was he alone? Did he proposition all the women who went to his room for a drink? Was she just one of many?

Got to concentrate! 'This latest outbreak of intestinal problems is getting out of hand. I would say about forty per cent of this week's tourists are now affected.'

'Would you like me to come over?'

Would she? 'If you're not too busy.'

'I've only got a short list of minor surgery this morning. Dr Afraz is perfectly capable of handling it so I'll be with you about...'

He paused, and she heard more tantalising sheet-rustling. At least he didn't seem to be conferring with anyone, but maybe he had his hand over the receiver.

'How about if I come for breakfast? If I move quickly I can catch the first seaplane.'

'That would be a good idea,' she said, in as nonchalant a voice as she could muster.

Putting down the phone, she rushed over to the wardrobe and carefully selected a clean cotton skirt and blouse. As she was finishing the final brushing and fixing of her long dark hair there was a tapping on her door.

She flung open the door and smiled when she saw her small friend from the village, standing on the threshold, a wide, friendly grin on his face.

'Musa! You're early today. Come in. How's your leg?'

'OK.'

Musa's English was limited, but adequate for short conversations. He'd told her he would like to learn English properly at school, but his parents couldn't afford to buy the uniform and shoes required to attend the village school.

Such a pity! Because he was obviously very bright. In the few weeks she'd been here she'd become very fond of him. Ever since she'd seen him having his leg stitched by Tim on that first morning in hospital, she'd grown to admire the sturdy boy. He was about eight years old, but it was difficult to believe he was that age because he was very small.

Soon after she'd met him in hospital he'd started coming to her room, asking if she had any rubbish she wanted him to dispose of. He had such a winning smile that she couldn't bring herself to refuse his help even though her room boy would have seen to it for her.

She handed Musa a small bag containing a couple of empty plastic water bottles and a paperback. Then she opened the fridge and took out a chocolate bar. It gave her such a nice feeling to see his little face light up with pleasure. This was the real purpose of the visit!

She watched him fondly, scampering off across the wooden walkway, until he disappeared along the sandy, leafy path that led back to the village. She was pleased to see that his leg wound wasn't causing him any problems.

As she sat at a veranda table outside the restaurant, watching the first seaplane of the day land on the water, Katie reflected that she must tell Tim how well his patient was doing. There was a deep scar on Musa's leg but it had healed beautifully.

She sipped her coffee as the seaplane came to a halt by the landing platform. The door of the plane opened, the steps were lowered and Tim appeared, stooping to get his tall frame through the door.

She smiled at the waiter hovering by her chair, indicating that she'd like another cup of coffee. Turning her eyes back to the landing platform to watch Tim board the *dhoni*, she sipped her coffee while she waited for him to arrive at the jetty.

A couple of minutes later he was coming towards her through the open sides of the restaurant veranda.

She felt the now-familiar rush of excitement at seeing him again. Calm down! she told herself. Stay cool. This is simply a professional situation. That warm, sensual encounter never happened.

'So, tell me about this latest outbreak,' he said, after they'd placed their order for fresh fruit, scrambled eggs and toast.

'Well, as you can see,' Katie said, gesturing with a sweep of her arm, 'the restaurant is half-empty. I've got patients who daren't leave their bathrooms, let alone their bungalows.'

Tim's face clouded over. 'We've never had anything like this on Kamafaroo before.'

Katie scooped up a piece of chilled papaya with her fork. 'I've got half a dozen severe cases in the hospital. I'm running all the usual tests on them, but so far the tests have been inconclusive.'

Tim chopped a piece of melon in half and squeezed mango juice over it. 'We'll have to question each one individually about what they've eaten and drunk while they've been here. I suggest you draw up a list of all the people affected.'

'I've done that.'

'Good. We'll share the list between us.'

He moved his fruit dish to one side and spooned scrambled eggs onto two plates from the serving bowl in the centre of the table.

'We'll need to look into the island plumbing situation,' he said, handing a plate of eggs to Katie. 'The restaurant kitchen must be checked and—' He broke off and gave her a wry smile. 'It's an endless list. Let's forget it for the moment and enjoy our breakfast.'

He leaned across the table and put his hand over hers. 'How've you been since I last saw you?' he said quietly.

Her pulse rate quickened at the touch of his fingers. 'Fine! Well, a bit shattered at first after Rick's revelations but I'm coming to terms with it.'

'That's good.'

He took away his hand and she found it easier to concentrate. She wanted to change the subject—she didn't want to think about Rick when she was with Tim.

She smiled at him across the table. 'It's such a beautiful island. I never stop marvelling at how lucky I am to be working here. And the village people are so friendly. Did I tell you that your little patient, Musa— the one who fell out of a tree—keeps coming to see me?'

He put down his fork and raised his eyes to hers. 'No, you didn't tell me. How is he?'

'He's fine. He'll always have a scar on that leg but I don't suppose he was planning to be a male model.'

Tim smiled at her. 'Does he just come for a chat?'

'I usually manage to find a bar of chocolate. He comes on the pretence of taking away my rubbish.'

'Your rubbish?'

'Oh, not just mine. I've seen him going along the path with rubbish bags from other bungalows. The tourists only give him their clean items, of course. Things like empty water bottles and paperback books.'

He gave her a wry grin. 'He probably sells the paperbacks in the village. Quite the little entrepreneur! But as for the water bottles... Oh, my God!'

Katie watched, disturbed, as she saw Tim clap a hand to his face.

He pushed his plate to one side. 'That could be it.'

She leaned forward clasping her hands together on the starched white tablecloth. 'What are you talking about?'

'The water bottles. Musa may be refilling them from some impure source and selling them to unsuspecting tourists.'

'Musa wouldn't do a thing like that!' she said indignantly. 'He wouldn't endanger the health of...' Her voice trailed away. Musa would be perfectly capable of refilling bottles and, at eight years old, it wouldn't occur to him that this was a dangerous practice.

'Musa doesn't realise that tourists from a different continent aren't immune to the organisms that are found in the water out here,' Tim said quietly. 'I'm not saying this is what is happening, but it's certainly a possibility.'

He pushed back his chair. 'Shall we go and find him?'

The narrow path to the village through the palm trees was shady. As Katie walked behind Tim she couldn't help admiring his tall, athletic frame. He was wearing well-pressed cotton shorts today so she could see the muscles in his long legs ripple as he moved forward.

He glanced back at her and, almost guiltily, she raised her eyes to his face.

He smiled. 'Not too hot?'

She smiled back. 'I'll survive.'

Why did he have to look at her in that tantalising way just when she was trying to get her feelings under control?

'Not much further.'

He turned to continue along the path. She breathed a sigh of relief, lifting her eyes to admire the tall, sturdy palm trees instead of the virile, male figure in front of her.

The path led into a clearing where several village houses were grouped around a central meeting point. A group of women from the village were chattering together as they dipped their buckets into the well. Small, brown-skinned babies played in the sand at their mothers' feet.

Tim turned to look down at Katie and together they mouthed the same words.

'The well!'

Katie pulled a wry face. The well could be the source of their problem if the tourists had, unwittingly, been drinking from it.

'Do you know which is Musa's house?' Tim asked her.

She shook her head. 'I'll ask someone.'

Approaching the laughing, chattering group, she enquired about Musa. One of the women pointed to a path leading out of the village.

Minutes later, as they came to the edge of the clearing, their suspicions were confirmed. Sitting outside one of the thatch-roofed dwellings, they saw Musa, who was concentrating all his energy on binding sticky tape around the plastic neck of a water bottle.

He looked up and waved happily as he saw them approaching.

'You like my shop?' he asked proudly, indicating the small table in front of him which was spread with a variety of items.

Katie looked down at the paperbacks, well-thumbed and splashed with suntan lotion, and the slices of coconut, beautifully arranged on palm leaves. But it was the row of plastic water bottles that alarmed her.

The little boy put his head on one side and gave them his most engaging smile. 'What you want to buy?

Tim leaned down and picked up one of the paper-backs. 'How much is this, Musa?'

The engaging smile broadened. 'One dollar.'

Katie noticed that Musa, like many of the Maldivian traders, chose to deal in US dollars, rather than the local currency of rufiyaa.

Tim put his hand in his pocket and pulled out a note, before squatting on the sand beside the little boy.

'You want water?' Musa asked.

'No, I don't want water,' Tim said slowly. 'Musa, you mustn't sell any more water to the tourists who come to the island.'

The little boy frowned as he tried to make sense of this seemingly ridiculous statement.

'Tourists want water. They pay too much at hotel. My water cheap. Good water from the well.'

Katie sank onto the sand beside Tim as they looked at each other, dismayed at the task of having to disillusion this well-intentioned child.

It took Tim several minutes of simple-worded elementary science to explain why the well water was OK for the people who'd been born on the island but dangerous for people from a long way away whose digestive systems reacted badly to the introduction of foreign organisms.

Musa was looking crestfallen. His mother had come out of the house with his two little brothers, one sitting on her hip and the other clinging to her hand. Katie listened to Tim explain again about the dangers inherent in unbottled water to Musa's mother. He was speaking in Divehi, the national language of the Maldive islanders, and he had an enviable fluency.

She herself was making an attempt to learn the rudiments of the language but it wasn't easy. She found it difficult to follow what Tim was saying.

'But I need money. I want to go to school,' Musa said plaintively. 'I need to buy good shirt and shoes.'

Tim put his hand in his shorts pocket. 'How much is the school uniform?' he asked Musa's mother.

She frowned, unable to understand what Tim was saying. Musa stepped in with a swift translation into his own language. As soon as she understood, the mother named the price.

Tim peeled off the requisite number of dollars and handed them to Musa's mother. 'This is for Musa's uniform,' he said clearly, before repeating what he'd said in Divehi. 'He must go to school. He's a very intelligent boy and he's wasting his most precious years by sitting around here.'

'I hate to see an intelligent boy like Musa getting a raw deal out of life,' Tim said, as they walked back along the path that led to the hospital. 'Education is so important.'

They'd reached the wide part of the path and were able to walk side by side. Katie glanced up at Tim and was touched by the earnest expression on his face.

'Do you think we've got our message through to Musa and his mother?'

Tim nodded. 'I'm sure we have. I didn't like having to tell him that the police would be called over from Male if he sold any more water, but I wanted him to realise how serious this was.'

'If he gets a good education he'll be able to make use of his obvious talents,' Katie said.

'For as long as I'm out here in the Maldives I'm going to help that family financially,' Tim said firmly. 'Education is vitally important. I mean, look at Rick. He started with nothing and he's reached his goal in life.'

Katie stopped in her tracks. 'Oh, come on, Tim. Let's not hold up Rick as an admirable example. He's used every trick in the book to get where he is today.'

'That's not entirely true,' Tim said, reaching to put his hands on her arms.

She looked up into his expressive eyes, feeling a shiver of sensual excitement at his close proximity. 'Why isn't it true? He's been an absolute scoundrel.'

'Yes, he walked out on you. He'd borrowed some money which he intended to pay back, but—'

'If you believe that, you'll—'

'Katie, you have to give him the benefit of the doubt! All this hatred is bad for you. If you don't get rid of it you'll poison any future relationship you might want to have.'

She remained motionless, knowing that she couldn't argue with that.

'But there are so many things that don't tie up,' she said quickly. 'Rick claims to have written to me, to have phoned me. I simply can't believe him!'

Tim's eyes flickered. 'Do you remember Rick telling us he'd spoken to your mother on the phone? According to him, she called him a rat before she put the phone down. How would he know your pet nickname if he'd hadn't contacted her?'

She felt a flicker of doubt creep in as she listened to Tim. Perhaps he was right. Rick couldn't have known they'd called him the Rat.

'Oh, God! I'm so confused, Tim!'

He pulled her against him. 'Let it go, Katie,' he said soothingly. 'What's past is past. It's not harming you any more, is it? Rick's even started paying you back.

You have to move forward in life...although it's easier said than done. In a way, I'm giving you the advice I find it hard to take myself.'

She felt his hands tighten on her arms.

'You mean Rebecca?' she asked quietly.

He nodded. 'It doesn't get any easier, but seeing the agonies you're putting yourself through has made me try to put my bad experience behind me.'

She took a deep breath. 'What exactly happened to—?'

'Not now, Katie,' he said brusquely. 'We need to get to the hospital and clear up this epidemic before it gets out of hand.'

As they walked on she tried to curb her curiosity, but it was impossible. She was now too involved with Tim not to care about his past.

Would he ever tell her about the mysterious Rebecca?

Sister Habaid was appalled when she heard what Tim had to say about the sale of water.

She turned to look at Katie, dismayed by the enormity of the problem. 'I can't believe the tourists could be so silly as to buy water from a village boy, can you, Doctor?'

'It's difficult to believe, but that's what's been happening,' Katie said, picking up the cup of coffee that Sister Habaid had prepared for her in her small office off the main entrance.

Tim stretched out his long legs in front of him, settled back in the cane armchair and looked across at Katie and Sister.

'The problem is that the tourists come out for one or two weeks only and they're very naïve. They explore the island and find themselves in the picturesque, quaint little village. What could be more endearing than a little boy selling bottled water? They have no reason to suspect the contents, especially as the tops are sealed.'

'That must be what happens,' Sister Habaid said thoughtfully, 'but it's got to be stopped.'

'I've put an end to it,' Tim said quickly. 'I'm certain that Musa won't do it again. He's agreed to get rid of all his water bottles. And I've persuaded his mother to send him to school. That should keep him fully occupied.'

He put down his coffee. 'Let's go and check on the tourists we've had to keep in hospital. I'd like to get them fit enough for their journey home.'

One ward had been filled with tourists, suffering from gastro-intestinal problems.

'You take this side of the ward, Katie,' Tim said. 'I'll take the opposite side.'

He turned to Sister Habaid who was hovering nearby. 'May we see the results of the pathological tests, Sister?'

Katie started her examination of the first patient in the ward. The drained, weary expression on the young woman's face showed that the days of suffering were taking their toll. When the body was losing too much fluid, dehydration could be a killer.

'You must drink plenty of water,' Katie said gently, lifting a glass to her patient's lips. 'If you don't keep on drinking to replace the fluids you've lost I'll have to put you on an intravenous drip. Have you been taking the pills I prescribed?'

The patient nodded.

'And, more important, have the pills stayed down?'

A flicker of a smile came over the young woman's lips. 'Yes, I haven't been sick for two days, Doctor. I think I'm on the mend.'

Katie patted her hand. 'So long as you keep drinking you'll be OK, Melanie. Another couple of days and you'll be back in your bungalow. If you take things easy you'll be able to enjoy the last part of your holiday.'

'I hope so. My boyfriend and I had planned to have the holiday of a lifetime. It's certainly been that!'

Halfway down the ward, Katie began examining a woman in her fifties. Her first impression was that the patient was excessively hot. She glanced at her chart. Janet Williams had been admitted that morning, suffering from severe intestinal pains.

'Show me where it hurts, Janet,' Katie said, after pulling round the cubicle curtains.

'Down here, Doctor…just about… Ah-h!'

Katie had been gentle but accurate in placing her fingers on the exact spot where the pain was, to the right side of the groin in the area known as the iliac fossa.

It could be symptomatic of this current epidemic or it could be something different. As she checked Janet's temperature the patient was violently sick. Katie held the bowl under her chin, knowing that she had to act fast. Holding open the curtain, she signalled to Tim who was across the ward.

'Janet has severe abdominal pain in the right iliac fossa and an extremely high temperature,' she said, showing him the patient's charts as soon as he arrived. 'The patient's age rules out the possibility of Fallopian tube pregnancy so it's more likely to be the appendix.'

Tim did a further examination, before straightening and nodding at Katie. 'I think you're right.'

He took her on one side, lowering his voice so that the patient couldn't hear. 'The excessive temperature is worrying. We'd better open her up before the appendix ruptures…if it hasn't already done so.'

'Have you ever worked in the theatre here?' Katie asked, recalling the simplicity of the operating theatre with some misgivings.

'It's adequate for emergencies,' he said quickly. 'If you prepare the patient I'll go and get the theatre ready.'

It was a very badly infected and swollen appendix that Tim removed from Janet Williams. As he dropped the offending organ into a swab receptacle his eyes met Katie's across the patient's motionless, gown-shrouded form.

'We were only just in time with this one,' he said.

'I'm glad you were here to do this operation,' Katie said in a relieved tone.

She saw the sides of his cheeks crinkle upwards and knew that he was smiling behind his mask.

'Oh, you'd have coped without me,' he said. 'You've got a good team here.'

He went on to praise Sister Habaid and the highly competent nurses grouped around the operating table.

As Katie listened to Tim's effusive thanks she wondered if she would have been brave enough to open up this little-used theatre. She'd assisted with general surgery in London, but the thought of working solo, albeit assisted by expert and devoted nursing staff, was very daunting.

She assisted him as he worked on the internal sutures. When it came to the external suturing of the skin he asked if she'd like to finish off. She nodded. Stitching patients was something she'd had lots of practice in. Her confidence returned as she secured the drainage tube in position, pulled the edges of the skin together and made a neat line of stitches.

Even though Tim was watching her carefully, she

didn't feel intimidated by him. Quite the reverse. He gave her a feeling of security. He was nodding his approval as she finished the last stitch.

'Keep Janet in Theatre until she comes round from the anaesthetic, Sister Habaid,' he said, turning to his ever-faithful assistant. 'When she's fully conscious you can take her back to the ward. I've written up the post-operative drugs. I'm staying on the island tonight so call the hotel reception if you need me. They'll know where to find me.'

For a fraction of a second Katie's mind wandered from the patient as she registered the fact that Tim was staying on the island. She could have handled any post-operative emergency herself, but it was nice to know that Tim would be on hand—in more ways than one!

Maybe she should invite him back for a drink? She could call it a sundowner and aim to be out on the veranda just as the sun slid down below the horizon.

It was perfect timing! The sun was, predictably, on form tonight as it threw a pink and gold iridescence over the sea, before finally sinking away beneath the waves.

For a couple of minutes neither of them spoke as they watched the pink and gold shades diffusing across the dimming sky.

'Beautiful!' Katie breathed.

'A perfect ending to a satisfying day,' Tim said quietly.

'I think I would have radioed for the emergency helicopter and had Janet transferred to Male,' Katie said, taking a sip of her orange juice. 'You were brilliant to be able to work under such primitive conditions.'

'Comes with practice,' he said. 'By the time the helicopter had got Janet to hospital the appendix would have perforated and peritonitis would have set in.'

Katie shivered as she thought about the consequences of peritonitis, a condition where the whole of the abdominal cavity was infected. It could be difficult to cure and sometimes proved fatal.

'I think I would have found the strength from somewhere to cope on my own,' she said, 'but I'm glad you were here all the same.'

He reached across and took one of her hands in his, touching the palm with gentle fingers.

'When emergencies happen the adrenalin flows and you get strength you didn't know you had. I've every confidence in you, Katie.'

She turned to look at him, the feel of his fingers on her hand unnerving her. His eyes were tender, his lips parted.

Was he waiting for her to make some sign that she wouldn't reject him? If so...

She leaned forward and he took her in his arms, his hands caressing her spine and sending tingling shivers down towards her bare feet. She crinkled her toes, revelling in the sensual waves that were creeping over her, gathering momentum with each movement of Tim's hands.

'Are you going to invite me inside?' he whispered. 'We'd be much more comfortable. Any minute now I'm going to slide off this chair and fall over the edge of your veranda into the sea. The fish might mistake me for their supper, don't you think?'

She giggled with relief. This was the sort of relationship she wanted. Light-hearted, sensual, yes; exciting, yes; but above all it had to be fun. Two people who admired each other, enjoying themselves together—living for the moment.

She smiled as she stood up and held out her hand. 'Come inside before the fish start getting wild ideas.'

Her room looked cosy in the dim illumination cast by the bedside lights. The room boy had been in to turn down her huge, kingsize bed while she'd been working at the hospital. The freshly laundered white sheets looked inviting.

Tim put a hand on her waist. She swung round and looked up into his expressive deep blue eyes. Slowly, oh, so slowly, he bent his head and kissed her, gently, on the lips.

She felt a shiver of desire shoot through her but for a moment she held herself rigid. The realisation dawned on her that she would be giving part of herself away if she succumbed to this longing to be in Tim's arms. She'd given in so easily to Rick and look how he'd treated her once he'd had her in his power.

Tim put a finger under her chin and tilted her face to look at him. 'I know what you're thinking,' he said quietly.

'No, you don't. I—!' She stopped in mid-outburst, alarmed by the ferocity of her own tone. 'At least, I hope you don't,' she added more quietly.

He held her against him and this time she didn't resist. As the familiar warm, sensuous feelings flooded over her she closed her eyes. Tim was utterly different to Rick. He wouldn't take advantage of her. He would—

'You're wondering whether you can trust me, aren't you?' As he said this, he was stroking her hair with one hand and caressing her spine with the other. Deep down inside she could feel waves of desire, welling up. It would be torture to resist such blissful temptation.

She drew in her breath as she looked up at those sensual lips, hovering so closely above her.

'Outside on the veranda we were simply being frivolous,' she began tentatively, 'but...'

She heard the wretched phone ringing but she ignored it. She wanted to explain to Tim exactly how she felt.

'We were living for the moment,' she continued carefully. 'Since we came inside the mood has changed, but I—'

He stooped and kissed her lightly, his eyes tender. 'Don't you think someone should answer the phone? It might be the hospital.'

He put an arm around her waist and pulled her with him across the bed as he reached for the phone. As she put her head down on his broad chest she was terribly aware of the thumping of his heart.

Mmm, it was going to be OK. All she had to do was suspend all thoughts about the past and the future. This was where she wanted to be now—with Tim, in his arms, enjoying his caresses and maybe, just maybe...

She was vaguely aware that his easy tone had changed. It was only when she heard him say that he would come at once that she tuned in to his conversation.

'OK, Sister Nasheedha. Don't worry. Just make sure that the patient doesn't move around in the bed before I arrive.'

Katie came back to earth as Tim pulled his arm away and stood up.

'What's the problem?'

'It's Janet Williams. Night Sister Nasheedha was changing her sheets and she thinks she might have disturbed the drainage tube.'

Katie felt a frisson of alarm shoot through her. 'But I

took great care to sew it in securely. I don't see how it could possibly have...'

He put his hands on her upper arms and looked down at her. Although there was still physical contact between them, he was the reassuring boss again, not the prospective lover.

'I know you did. It's probably a false alarm but I'd better go. Sister Nasheedha has a tendency to panic easily.'

'Shall I come with you?'

He shook his head. 'No, get some sleep. I'll see you in the morning.'

She saw him striding across her room. As the door closed she ran to the window and peeped through the blinds to watch him cross the wooden walkway. A night owl, sitting in a palm tree, puffed out its feathers and uttered its distinctive cry as Tim walked beneath it.

As he disappeared into the thick, dark green, tropical foliage that flanked the path to the hospital she turned back into the room, looking longingly at the bed.

Well, she'd certainly blown it tonight! Of all the idiotic ways to pour cold water on what could have been a wonderful experience with a man she admired so much.

No, it was more than admiration. Her feelings were developing into something unique.

Was it love? Was she falling in love?

She shivered, and her fingers turned automatically to switch off the air conditioning. She needed warming up. She wanted to be in Tim's arms.

Next time...if there was a next time...she would keep control of her destructive inhibitions, she promised herself as she went out onto the veranda. The warm sea air revived her flagging spirits. She sank into the chair where Tim had sat, leaned back against the hollow in the cushion made by his rugged body and gazed out across the sea.

Over there, on Fanassi, Rick would be enjoying himself. It was time for her to shake off the past and move on into the future.

Would Tim see her light and call back after he'd been to the hospital?

CHAPTER SIX

'THERE was absolutely nothing to worry about,' Tim said, as he examined the abdominal area around their patient's drainage tube. 'Apparently, there was some movement when Night Sister changed the bottom sheet but the stitches held the tube in place.'

Katie leaned across from the other side of the bed to get a better look at her handiwork.

'Nice stitches,' Tim commented, with a wry smile.

She looked across into his eyes, those eyes which had been so full of tenderness last night just before she'd thrown a wobbly and done them both out of what would surely have been a blissful experience.

Life was too short to agonise over whether she should ever feel deeply again. She knew from her feelings last night that she could easily get carried away. With someone as wonderful as Tim, wasn't it worth taking a risk?

She smiled back at him. 'So Sister Nasheedha needn't have called you out, then?'

'No, I could have stayed on.'

She took a deep breath. 'You could have come back.'

Had she really said that? She was being far too provocative by half! And in front of a patient. How unprofessional could you get?

'How does your tummy feel now, Janet?' she asked, moving back up the bedside to return to being a proper doctor.

Janet Williams turned her grey-haired head on the pillow to look at Katie. 'It's a bit sore, but I'll survive. My husband's supposed to be coming in this morning, but I expect he's still asleep.'

'Well, he is on holiday after all,' Tim said.

'So am I,' Janet said, with a hint of bitterness, 'but it doesn't much feel like it at the moment. Anyway, thank you both for all you've done for me. Sister Nasheedha said I might have died if you two hadn't operated.'

'Sister Nasheedha tends to exaggerate,' Tim said quickly. 'You're going to be fine.'

They were finishing their morning round of the hospital. Katie was relieved to find a distinct improvement in the patients with gastro-intestinal problems. She'd assured most of them that they could return to their bungalows in a day or two.

'I'd better go and start my morning surgery,' she said, as they walked out into the corridor.

'And I've got to get back to Male,' he told her evenly.

A distinct feeling of loss crept over her, like a cloud obscuring the sun. When would she see him again? They hadn't made any plans to get together.

'You didn't answer my question,' she said, amazed at her own boldness. Desperate situations required desperate measures!

'I didn't know you'd asked a question,' he said.

She detected a hint of amusement in his voice. He was enjoying playing hard to get. They'd reached her surgery door. Any moment now he would stride away. She had to speak out before it was too late.

'In the ward just now I said you could have come back last night, as there was nothing wrong with Janet's drainage tube.'

She looked up at him and saw that his eyes were twinkling. He was leaning languidly against the wall beside the door she'd just opened.

He grinned. 'That wasn't a question—that was a statement.'

'Oh, Tim! Stop being so pedantic!'

She reached out and took hold of the front of his shirt. The intense heat had already dampened it with sweat.

'Why didn't you come back when you discovered there wasn't an emergency?' she asked, all in a rush, before she could stop herself. She watched as a surprised expression flitted across his eyes.

'I didn't know you wanted me to come back,' he said slowly.

She took her hand from his shirt and dropped it to her side. 'Neither did I,' she said quietly, 'until it was too late.'

A couple of nurses were coming towards them down the corridor, watching them with avid interest.

'Then we'll have to rectify the situation, Dr Mandrake,' Tim said in a professional voice. 'I'll give the problem my urgent attention but I'll need your help.'

The nurses had disappeared round the corner of the corridor. Katie could hear their chattering voices getting fainter.

'Why don't you come over to Male one evening?' Tim said, reverting to his normal voice now that there were no eavesdroppers. 'Sunday's usually quiet here in hospital so they could easily manage without you. We could have a meal and—'

'You mean this Sunday?'

'Any reason why not?'

'No. Sunday would be fine.'

In actual fact, it would be perfect! Sunday was Valentine's Day and also her birthday, but Tim wouldn't know that. Valentine's Day wouldn't have registered with him out here in the Maldives and he wasn't to know it was her birthday. She certainly wouldn't tell him, but she would secretly enjoy the experience of being with him on her own special day.

He glanced at his watch. 'Got to dash. I've got a long theatre list this morning.'

'In a proper theatre,' Katie remarked, aware that she was clinging to his last moments with her.

He smiled. 'Hi-tech stuff this morning. So, shall I see you on Sunday?'

'If I can escape,' she said lightly, not wanting Tim to think she was a push-over. She'd been uncharacteristically brazen this morning. Now was the time to hold back a bit and let him do the running.

'Six o'clock at my place. OK?'

'I'll be there as soon as I can. If there's a problem at the hospital I may be a bit late.'

He waved a hand as he disappeared round the corner of the corridor. She went into her surgery and sat down. Buzzing on the intercom, she asked Nurse Sabia to come and see her.

Seconds later Nurse Sabia came through the door that led directly into the reception area. Katie could see the patients who were waiting for her. Not as many as usual, but it was still early and also she had an unusual number of tourists as inpatients. There couldn't be many tourists left in their bungalows.

Nurse Sabia was carrying a pile of case notes. Tim had told Katie they'd tried to introduce a computerised system but it hadn't worked. Everyone on Kamafaroo preferred sheets of paper to flickering screens. And the frequent power cuts had finally convinced Tim that he should abandon the computer project.

'Good morning, Nurse Sabia.'

'Good morning, Doctor. Are you ready to take the first patient? I think she should be seen quickly.'

'Of course. What's the problem?'

'She was swimming off the reef this morning and she got bitten by a large fish.'

Katie frowned. This was the first time she'd ever had to deal with a case of fish bite. 'You'd better bring her in.'

Nurse Sabia nodded, her long, black, shining hair gleaming in the morning sunlight that streamed through the windows. At the door she turned. 'You must tell her not to feed the fish again, Doctor.'

'Why?' Katie was confused.

'Because if you feed the fish they follow you, and when you have no more food to give them they sometimes like to nibble at your skin. People who are born here on Kamafaroo know this. Tourists sometimes don't.'

'To be honest, I hadn't heard this either, Nurse. Thank you for telling me.'

Nurse Sabia inclined her head and moved swiftly out into the reception area, to return seconds later with a tall, well-built, blonde woman who might have been forty or in her late thirties.

'This is Helen McGuire, Doctor,' Nurse Sabia said, opening the appropriate sheaf of notes for Katie to scan.

'Do sit down, Mrs McGuire.'

'Call me Helen, Doctor,' the patient said, sinking into the chair at the side of Katie's desk.

Looking at the well-upholstered frame of her patient, Katie could see why the fish might have mistaken her for food. A wide cotton bandage, with blood seeping through, was tied round her upper arm.

'Tell me what happened,' Katie said, as she started to unwrap the bandage.

'I was swimming out near the edge of the reef when this large fish started following me. I swam a bit faster but it took a bite at my arm.'

With the bandage off, Katie could see the extent of the damage. A gash, which extended from the left shoulder almost to the elbow, was bleeding.

Carefully, she swabbed the raw area with cetavalon, before suturing the sections which gaped open.

'I'm going to start you on antibiotics, Helen,' Katie said, handing over a couple of tablets and a glass of water. 'This will help to prevent any infection setting in.'

'Thanks, Doctor,' her patient said, setting the glass of water back on the desk. 'I've never been bitten by a fish before.'

Katie leaned back in her chair. 'Nurse Sabia just told me that it was probably because you were feeding the fish.'

Helen McGuire looked puzzled. 'I don't see what that has to do with it.'

'Well, it's the first time I've heard about it but, apparently, the fish mistake you for food when you stop feeding them. They like to check out if you're worth swallowing.'

'I'd never thought of that, Doctor.'

'Neither had I, but everyone born on Kamafaroo understands not to feed the fish. You were unlucky that no one had told you about it.'

The rest of her morning was totally taken up with her outpatients but she found time for a swim during the afternoon, before returning to the hospital to check on

Janet Williams and the other tourist inpatients. It was satisfying to find that there were no further medical problems and that all her gastro-enteritis patients were improving.

As she walked back to her bungalow along the sandy path she looked up at the moon and, for an instant, had an overwhelming sense of loneliness. Here she was on this idyllic island and no one to share its beauty with her. Her eyes automatically looked out towards the sea, towards the bright lights of Male on the horizon.

She walked briskly across the wooden walkway, telling herself to snap out of it. Life was pretty good at the moment. For four years she'd been totally independent and she didn't need to surrender her independence to anybody. A light fling would be OK but—

Was that the phone? She fumbled madly with the key in the door... Oh, come on, turn you stupid thing! Why were her fingers all thumbs when the phone call might be from...?

'Oh, hi, Tim.'

She flung herself down on the bed, the phone held in the crook of her shoulder, pleased that she'd been able to keep her tone decidedly nonchalant.

'You sound breathless.'

'I've just got in. The phone was ringing and I thought...I thought it might be the hospital.'

'How about taking the whole day off on Sunday? I've cleared it here in Male. I think they should be able to cope without you for a few hours.'

'You're the boss.' She took a deep breath. 'What did you have in mind?'

'I thought I could come over to Kamafaroo on Sunday morning, help you with your morning round of the hospital and then we could take the rest of the day off. We could start with a swim off your veranda and take it from there.'

'Sounds good to me.'

She leaned back against the pillow and squeezed the phone, imagining for a moment that it was Tim's hand. What a perfect way to spend her birthday and Valentine's Day!

'Anything to report on Janet Williams?'

Tim sounded as if he was being deliberately professional again.

'Drainage tube still *in situ*. She won't need it much longer. The wound's drying up nicely.'

'Good.'

Long pause... How could she keep him talking...?

He cleared his throat. 'I'll see you on Sunday morning.'

'Yes.'

'Goodnight, Katie. Sweet dreams.'

She certainly hoped she would have sweet dreams as she put down the phone and started counting the days to her Valentine's Day date.

'I think the sea looks exceptionally calm simply because I've got the rest of the day off,' Katie said, rolling over onto her back so that she could lie on the surface of the water.

Tim laughed. 'I can't see the logic of that but perhaps it's not a logical sort of day. Too hot to think.'

He swam towards her and splashed water over her face.

'Ouch!' She turned over and started to chase him as he swam quickly away from her.

They'd finished their morning round of the hospital and were taking a swim before a late breakfast.

Suddenly he slowed and she caught up with him. She sensed that he was waiting for her. Languidly, he put out his arm and drew her towards him. His face was close now and his lips parted.

She trod water as he leaned towards her and kissed her lightly.

'Happy Sunday!' he said softly.

She laughed as she splashed her feet in the water. This was as good as being wished a happy birthday. As no one on the island knew it was her birthday it was unlikely that—

'And happy birthday,' he whispered, his lips against her ear.

Her eyes widened with surprise. 'How on earth did you know it was my birthday?'

He laughed. 'I remembered it from when I had to check your application form. Your date of birth was there so it's the big three-oh, isn't it? Congratulations!'

She flipped over onto her back again and gazed up at the cloudless blue sky. 'Was that why you suggested I had a day off?'

He moved closer. 'That had something to do with it, yes.'

Her thoughts were in a whirl. 'Come on, let's go and have some breakfast before they close the dining room. Race you back to my place.'

He was close behind her all the way but at the last moment, as they reached the metal ladder leading up to her veranda, he swam easily past her to stand on the lowest rung and hold out his hand.

Sea water was dripping from his chest. He was smiling at her, his eyes expressively alive with the excitement of the moment.

As she took hold of his outstretched fingers it was as

if there was a current of electricity running between them. He held back so that she could go up the steps and climb onto the veranda first.

'Hey, what's this?'

She looked in amazement at the white-clothed table, the silver-covered chafing dishes, the fresh fruit and the huge cafetière of coffee. In the centre of the wooden veranda table was a single red rose. She turned to look at Tim as he reached the top step.

'Who did...?'

He gave her a rakish grin. 'I ordered room service, special occasion breakfast menu. That's why I made sure we were swimming round the corner when the waiter came to set it out.'

'Oh, how...how romantic!'

The word slipped out and she wished she'd chosen another one. She didn't want Tim to think she was lining him up as a potential candidate for a real romance.

He was standing very close to her now, and beads of water were beginning to dry on his skin. She was very much aware of the virile shape of his body, clad only in the briefest of swimwear.

'Did you know it was Valentine's Day?' he asked, one eyebrow raised, as if trying to keep the moment light.

'Well, yes, because my birthday is on Valentine's Day.' She gave a nervous laugh. 'My mum told me it was the first Valentine's Day she'd had to spend in hospital and she hoped it would be the last.'

She broke off. 'Here, have a towel.' She handed him a large white, fluffy towel, wrapping herself in another one. Being so close to Tim, wearing only her bikini, made her feel decidedly vulnerable.

'Would you like to have first shower?' she asked, continuing in her role of hostess.

'No, thanks. I'm starving! Let's have breakfast.'

He moved quickly to pull out one of the chairs from the table. 'If madame would care to join me?'

She laughed as she saw him whip his towel over one arm and adopt a waiter-like pose, his head on one side and his eyes sparkling mischievously. Tying her own towel, sari-style, around her, she sat down in the chair that Tim was holding out. His fingers brushed the back of her naked shoulders and a frisson of excitement ran down her spine.

She watched in animated anticipation as he settled himself opposite her and began to take the covered lids off the various dishes.

'Would madame care for some scrambled egg?'

'Yes, please.'

'With mushrooms, tomatoes…?'

She said yes to everything he offered her. The early morning work in hospital and the exhilarating swim had given her a healthy appetite. And just looking across at Tim, with the sun streaming across the veranda, gave her the feeling that she hadn't been so happy for a long time.

Was it just being with Tim or was it the idyllic setting—the sparkling blue sea, the warmth of the sun, the brilliant parade of tropical fish swimming beneath and around the veranda? Would she feel so happy to breakfast with Tim if they were in freezing cold London?

A large grey and white heron swooped down to scoop a fish from the water, carrying it in its beak high into the sky before veering back towards the island. Life wasn't idyllic for all the creatures around here, but for her, at this precious moment, it couldn't be better.

But it couldn't last. Sooner or later…

'Why are you looking so serious all of a sudden?'

'Am I?' She scooped some scrambled egg onto her fork. 'This scrambled egg is delicious.'

'You didn't answer my question. One minute you looked as if you were in heaven and the next the storm clouds had appeared. Was it something I said?'

She put down her fork and faced him across the table. This man seemed to be able to read her like a book!

'I was thinking how happiness is so transient. It comes and goes. Sometimes without warning and—'

'I know exactly what you mean.'

He reached across and put his hand over hers. 'Sometimes, just when you think life couldn't be better, your world collapses around you.'

She held her breath. His face had a solemn expression she hadn't seen before. Was he finally going to divulge some of his past experiences to her? She mustn't speak, mustn't intrude on his thoughts…

'I thought I'd got everything I wanted in life when I put a diamond ring on Rebecca's finger,' Tim said, quietly in a far-away voice.

She watched him from across the table as he turned to gaze out over the blue expanse of sea, hardly daring to breathe in case he clammed up again on this sensitive subject.

'We were working together in the ship's hospital on a round-the-world cruise. We'd known each other for about a year, meeting up on various ships. Sometimes, if we were working on different ships, we'd arrange to meet for a brief weekend in some exotic location.' He broke off and she waited. Dare she prompt him to continue his story?

She took a deep breath. 'It sounds idyllic. So what happened to spoil it all?'

He turned his eyes back from the sea and she saw the poignant expression on his face.

'On this final assignment, working together, we'd planned to marry in the Caribbean. We were carrying a relief doctor who would take over from me so we could leave the ship for our honeymoon. Hugh seemed a pleasant young doctor, newly qualified but very competent. We all got on well together until…'

He paused and she waited.

'A couple of weeks before we were due to marry I was called out in the middle of the night to see an elderly woman who'd suffered a stroke. I got her into our ship's hospital, before phoning Rebecca to come and give me a hand.'

He sucked in air between his teeth as if unable to continue. For a moment Katie waited silently, but the suspense was unbearable.

'And did she?'

'There was no answer from her cabin. I phoned Hugh—no reply. I settled my patient and went along to Rebecca's cabin. On the way there I passed Hugh's cabin. His light was on. I could hear voices. One of them was Rebecca's.'

'And…?'

'I knocked on the door. After a couple of minutes Hugh opened it. He tried to close it again when he saw it was me but I forced my way inside. I had to know if something was going on.'

'And was it?'

He nodded. 'Rebecca was lying on the bed and it was obvious that they… I wanted to lash out at Hugh, to knock him down, but fortunately my senses hadn't totally deserted me. Even though I was so furious that I could hardly speak, something held me back. I reasoned that Rebecca had gone to Hugh's cabin of her own accord so that was the end of our relationship as far as I was concerned.'

He stood up and went over to the edge of the veranda, gripping the rail with tightening fingers as he looked down into the sea.

'I didn't want her back even though she came along and pleaded with me afterwards. Said she was sorry, got carried away, hadn't meant it to happen.'

Katie pushed back her chair and moved across the veranda to stand beside him. He put out an arm and gathered her against his side.

'And the ring, the diamond engagement ring you gave Rebecca—did she give it back to you?'

He looked down at her, a surprised expression on his face. 'Never gave it a thought. I just wanted to be rid of her.'

'That's exactly how I felt about Rick,' Katie said quietly. 'Material things don't matter when you've lost faith in somebody you thought you loved.'

They stood together for a few highly charged moments, looking down at the fish weaving in and out of the coral, before Tim spoke again in a low husky voice.

'So, you see, we've both suffered because of partners who let us down. Which is one reason why we get on so well together, don't you think?'

She raised her eyes to his. 'You mean we've both been through the agony so—'

'So we both know we wouldn't want to experience that again,' he said quickly. 'After the Rebecca trauma I vowed I'd never get so heavily involved again. I don't intend to be a monk but commitment and marriage are out as far as I'm concerned. How about you?'

'Oh, yes. I entirely agree,' she said, a little too quickly. 'After Rick I felt like going into a nunnery!'

He laughed and his laughter broke the tension. He tightened his arm around her waist.

'I'm glad you didn't go into a nunnery. I might never have met you and... Come on, let's finish our breakfast. I almost forgot the champagne.'

He disappeared inside her room to return with a bottle of champagne in an ice bucket.

'I told the waiter to leave this inside in the air conditioning. There's some orange juice as well so that we can make it into Buck's fizz if you prefer. I'll take mine neat to toast your birthday.'

'Me, too!'

He popped the cork and poured out two glasses. 'Happy birthday, Katie!' He came round the table. 'And happy Valentine's Day!'

As she looked up into those infinitely blue eyes, watching her with such tenderness, she sensed it would be the best Valentine's Day she'd ever spent.

It was such a pity this would be the only one she'd spend with Tim. He'd made it quite clear that their relationship was to be light and transient. Well, that was what she wanted, too, wasn't it?

'Your phone's ringing.'

She took another sip of the delicious champagne, before putting down her glass.

'Hope it's not the hospital,' she said as she crossed the veranda.

'Don't worry. I've asked Dr Afraz to come over from Male and spend the day here. He was due on the mid-morning plane so he should be on call already.'

As she picked up the phone, Katie couldn't help marvelling at how organised Tim was. Besides the birthday breakfast, he'd even arranged cover for her day off. Who knew what treats were in store for the rest of the day?

'Happy birthday, darling!'

'Mum! What a lovely surprise!'

'Mustn't talk long. It's fiendishly expensive. How are you, darling?'

'I'm fine. It's a very interesting job.'

'And your love life?'

'Oh, Mum! What makes you think I—?'

'Call it sixth sense. You sound sort of…happy.'

'I am happy, but there doesn't have to be a man in my life to make me happy. I'm an independent career girl, remember?'

Oh, heavens! Tim had just opened the casement door from the veranda and was padding barefoot across the room, signalling that he'd like to take a shower.

'Is that OK?' he was asking, from the other side of her room.

She nodded and mouthed, 'Yes.'

'Katie, is someone with you?'

'Just a friend.' The bathroom door was now firmly shut. She breathed a sigh of relief. 'A colleague, actually.'

Remembering that the phone call had to be brief, she hurried on. 'Mum, I've seen Rick and he's started to pay back the money he owes me. Apparently, he tried to phone me and sent me a letter. You don't by any chance know if—'

'Darling, I did it for your sake.'

Katie frowned and sat down on the bed, curling her fingers round the cord of the phone. 'Did what for my sake?'

She heard her mother make an impatient clicking of her tongue, before explaining, 'Do you remember when you came home for a holiday soon after Rick left you?'

How could she possibly forget those agonising weeks? 'Yes, it was the holiday time I'd earmarked for my honeymoon.'

'Well, he phoned. Rick phoned while you were in the garden one day and—'

'But why didn't you call me in?'

'It was for your own good, Katie. I told him he was a rat to leave you like that...'

So she *had* called him a rat! He'd been telling the truth.

'And that he wasn't to contact you again. Just to make sure he didn't, I told him that you'd been so traumatised you'd left your job and come to live at home.'

'Mum! Why on earth...?'

'I keep telling you, Katie, I know more about men than you do. I was trying to protect you. If he'd contacted you at the hospital you might have taken him back.'

'Oh, no, I wouldn't! I would never have let him come back.' Light was beginning to dawn. 'So, if Rick thought I was living at home, is it possible he might have sent a letter to me at my home address?'

There was a slight pause. 'It's possible.'

Katie ploughed on relentlessly with her interrogation. 'So, the letter Rick told me he'd sent might not have reached me, perhaps?'

'That's possible too.' Pause. 'Look, Katie, I knew the letter was from Rick—it had his name and address on the back—so I put it straight in the bin.'

'You didn't open it?'

'Of course not! I would never dream of opening your letters!'

Katie couldn't help smiling. Her mother's logic never ceased to mystify her!

The sound of splashing water in the shower room had stopped. Any moment now Tim would emerge.

'Mum, I'd better not run up your phone bill. Thanks ever so much for calling.'

'And you're not mad at me?'

'Of course not. You thought you were doing the right thing.'

'Goodbye, darling. Take care of yourself. Don't forget to use a good sun cream. You don't want to get wrinkles now you're thirty.'

'Goodbye, Mum.'

She put down the phone as Tim came through from the shower room. One sun-tanned hand was rubbing a towel over his hair, the other tucking his shirt into his swim pants. He'd carried a sports bag, containing his swimming gear and a change of clothes, into the shower room when he first arrived.

'So you're an independent career girl,' he said, with an amused smile. 'Good for you!'

She laughed. 'Oh, I had to say something. You know how mothers like to quiz you about your love life.'

He shrugged. 'I don't, actually. I left home when I was sixteen.'

'But you told me you'd had this predictable childhood. Your parents were doctors and—'

'I was a bit of a rebel. I got tired of the predictability. I was expected to become a doctor. I could see my life running along in a groove, like my parents and my grandparents. So when I was sixteen I left home, took my post office savings money, bought a one-way ticket to Bombay and travelled around for a couple of years.'

'A rolling stone gathers no moss,' she said lightly. 'But how did you live?'

'You can live cheaply in the East. I took a variety of jobs when I needed money. For a while I worked in a hotel, waiting tables—that was a good job because I got my food as well.'

'And you did this for a couple of years?'

He nodded. 'Until I'd got the travel bug out of my system. When I was eighteen I decided that I couldn't live like this for the rest of my life. I'd saved up enough for a ticket back to the UK. I decided I wanted to be a doctor after all.'

'So you went back home?'

'Not exactly. I went back to the UK and phoned my parents. They said they wouldn't help me. They were furious because I'd dropped out of school. So I took various jobs in London, went to classes in the evening until I'd passed the required exams to apply for medical school, and—' He broke off with a wry grin. 'I didn't mean this to turn into a documentary on my life.'

He was going towards the veranda. 'Come and finish your glass of champagne before it goes flat.'

As she followed him she said, 'It couldn't have been easy for you, having to be self-sufficient at such a young age.'

'It was tough at times, but it was what I'd chosen. I was sorry I'd upset my parents but there was nothing I could do since they refused to see me. After a few years in hospital I started travelling again. There were no family ties to keep me in the UK.'

'But didn't your parents relent? They must have been proud when you passed your finals and became—'

'My parents were killed in a car crash during my final year.'

'Oh... I'm so sorry. I—'

'That's life, isn't it? No going back. Just learning from experience.'

She looked out across the sea. For a few minutes neither of them spoke, both wrapped up in their own thoughts. It was Katie who broke the silence.

'I've solved the mystery of Rick's phone call and letter.' Tim's eyes widened as she explained what her mother had told her.

'Maternal instinct does strange things to some women,' he said quietly. 'I suppose your mother thought she was protecting you.'

'That's how I've rationalised it, but I wish I'd known sooner. I wouldn't have been so consumed with hate that—' She broke off. She must try to forget.

'One good thing came out of it,' he said, as he took another sip of champagne. 'Perhaps, if you hadn't been so obsessed by Rick's rotten behaviour, you might not have come out to the Maldives and—'

'And I wouldn't have been sitting on a sunlit veranda in the Indian Ocean, sipping champagne,' she put in lightly.

'I was going to say we wouldn't have met.'

His voice was husky, his eyes tender as he reached across and took hold of her hand. Looking at the expression on his face, she found it hard to believe that here was a man who'd vowed never to feel deeply about anyone again. He looked perfectly capable of going completely overboard!

She sensed that it was going to be very difficult to resist her feelings where Tim was concerned. Her mind was telling her to keep a grip on herself but her heart was all for giving in to her emotions.

The phone was ringing again. It was the dining room, asking if they could send a waiter to clear the breakfast.

Tim suggested a walk on the beach while the bungalow was being serviced. 'No need to get dressed,' he said. 'We can stay in our swim togs.'

The sand was too hot for their bare feet so they paddled through the shallows. Shoals of small tropical fish swam near the shore. Every now and again there would be a whooshing sound and some of the fish would leap into the air in an attempt to escape the jaws of a hungry bigger fish.

'We'll take the afternoon plane to Male so I can show you round the town,' Tim said, as they sheltered from the sun under a palm tree on their way back to Katie's room.

'I'd like that,' she said. 'I've been planning to explore the streets of Male ever since I arrived in the Maldives, but I've never found the time. Can't take too much time off. I've got a tough boss.'

He laughed. Reaching out, he took a handful of sand and sprinkled it slowly over her bare legs. As the grains of sand trickled down between her toes she gave an involuntary shiver. Even without touching her, this man could ignite flickers of desire deep down inside her.

She pulled herself to her feet. 'We'd better get ready if we're to catch that plane.'

The sand was scorching under her feet. She began to run. The sooner she got back and took a shower to quell the surge of warm sensations inside her the better!

As she walked through the door she saw that her bed had been made with freshly laundered sheets and turned

down at both corners. She tried not to look at it, feeling
suddenly very much aware of Tim close behind her.

'I need to shower before I change,' she said, in a
matter-of-fact tone.

'So do I.'

She looked up at him, unnerved by the enigmatic expression on his face. 'Well, I'll go first and then you
can...'

He was pulling her against him. 'We could shower
together,' he said, with a rakish grin. 'Much more fun.'

She hadn't thought of a shower as being fun before.
It was a means of cleansing and cooling her hot, damp
body. But as Tim's hands began to caress her bare arms
the idea took on a whole new meaning.

As if in a dream, she found herself being propelled
into the shower room. Tim's hands were removing her
bikini. Sand was being scattered over the newly washed
tiles. Amazingly, she found herself reaching out towards
Tim, and without a trace of embarrassment she un-
hooked the fastening on his swim pants.

For an instant they stood together, holding each other,
revelling in the feel of skin against skin.

He turned on the shower and the warm water cascaded
over them. He was laughing now as he poured shower
gel over her, rubbing his hands over her skin. His laughter was infectious. She joined in the hilarious game, relieved to find that she'd lost all her inhibitions. It seemed
perfectly natural that the two of them should be together
like this. They were like two water babies, playing together in a rainstorm.

And then, suddenly, his lips were on hers and she felt
herself go limp with sensual desire. The laughter and
fun were still there but a deeper, more passionate mood
was taking over. She knew, without a shadow of a doubt,

that there could only be one conclusion to this mad, spur-of-the-moment game of make-believe.

And at that moment she wanted this conclusion more than anything in the world. It was something that had to happen between them—it was almost as if it had been pre-ordained. Fate had brought them to this idyllic island so that they could enjoy being together for a short time before they resumed their real lives somewhere else.

Tim turned off the shower and gently, oh, so gently, wrapped her in a towel, before lifting her in his arms and carrying her over to the bed.

None of this felt real. As she lay, watching the towel fall from Tim's waist, she shivered with delicious anticipation. He had such a superb body. She'd never been able to appreciate how handsome he was when his muscular frame was clothed. But now...he looked utterly magnificent as he climbed onto the bed and took her in his arms.

Their bodies were still damp from the shower as they clung to each other. His caressing hands were arousing a longing for fulfilment. At first he was gentle with her and then, as if sensing her aroused desires, his caresses strengthened until their love-making surged towards an ecstatic climax.

Afterwards, Katie lay panting in Tim's arms, a feeling of dizzy unreality sweeping over her. Her tingling body felt utterly spent and satisfied. She turned on her side and saw that Tim was watching her with a wary expression on his face.

'I didn't plan this to happen,' he said huskily. 'I hope you don't think I set up a champagne scenario just to get you into bed.'

She put a finger over his mouth. 'Shush. I wanted it

too, otherwise I wouldn't have gone along with it. I'm a very independent woman, as you well know.'

He laughed. 'As you'll never let me forget. Well, that's OK, then. Let's have another glass of champagne to celebrate your thirtieth birthday.'

'Don't keep reminding me how old I am,' she said, as she watched him walk naked across the room to the fridge, returning with the champagne bottle and two fresh glasses.

It seemed strange to return to everyday talk after their tempestuous love-making. Just thinking about it sent sensual shivers down her spine. But it seemed as if they were going to be able to put it behind them and continue with their normal lives.

Had it been a one-off event? She certainly hoped not! Looking at Tim now as he poured out the champagne, she could almost imagine she was falling in love with him.

Who was she kidding? She took the glass from his fingers and sipped the ice-cold liquid. It might cool her fingers but deep down inside her she was still on fire. She was in love with this tantalising man and there wasn't anything she could do about it.

She told herself she was glad he'd been wearing a condom. Safe sex was something she always advocated when discussing the subject with her patients. But for a split second she'd felt almost cheated. Did he always carry condoms with him? Who else did he take to bed?

She closed her eyes, banishing her jealous thoughts as she lay back against the pillows. Jealousy must play no part in this relationship. It was a transient, fun situation and she mustn't allow herself to get serious. Neither of them must get hurt when it finished. It mustn't end in tears.

As Tim put his arm around her shoulders and drew her against him, they heard a droning sound above them.

He laughed. 'That's the afternoon plane we planned to catch. Oh, well, we'll have to take the speedboat.'

'But that doesn't leave until—' She broke off as she saw the wickedly sensual smile on his lips. He was running his fingers through her hair.

'Thank goodness for that,' he whispered. 'I'd hate to have to cut short your birthday party. We've got all afternoon so...'

The evening shadows were falling through the louvred windows when she awoke. Turning on her side, she saw that Tim was looking down at her with a tender expression.

'I was just about to waken you. We'll have to get a move on if we're to catch the speedboat.'

Looking at the rumpled sheets, she remembered their passionate lovemaking which had become more and more feverish and infinitely more satisfying. This was one relationship she would find very difficult to relinquish.

She watched as Tim padded across the wooden floor to the shower room. This time she wouldn't follow him. If she did they wouldn't have a hope of catching the boat!

Returning with wet hair, he moved across and took her in his arms.   'I think St Valentine would approve of the way we're spending his day, don't you?' he whispered.

She looked up into his eyes. 'Absolutely!'

She swallowed hard as she remembered that Valentine's Day was meant for real lovers, planning a future together, not for a couple like Tim and herself who were having a temporary relationship.

The narrow streets of Male were fascinating, still alive with traders even during the late evening. In the sector called the Singapore Bazaar there were rows of colourful and quaint little shops. Tim took her arm and steered her inside one of the shops which had jewellery in the window.

She admired the trays of old silver and antique jewellery which had been imported from India and Sri Lanka. Some of the jewellery made in the Maldives had been fashioned out of coral, she noticed.

'I want you to choose something for your birthday,' Tim said.

'That's pretty,' she said, picking up an inexpensive coral necklace.

'Don't take that,' Tim said. 'We mustn't encourage the depletion of coral in the islands. Choose something made from silver. How about this one?'

He held an antique silver necklace against her throat. 'That looks lovely. Do you like it?'

It was an exquisite piece of jewellery. She adored it!

'I think it's very beautiful,' she said carefully, 'but it's also very expensive and—'

'Not for a combined birthday and Valentine's Day present,' he said, handing a wad of dollars over the counter to the delighted proprietor of the shop. 'Don't wrap it. The lady will wear it tonight.'

She swallowed hard as Tim fastened the clasp behind her neck. The shopkeeper produced a mirror.

'It's...exquisite,' she said, trying to hang on to her emotional response. 'Thank you so much.'

She really shouldn't be accepting expensive presents

from Tim but…she could always give it back when it was all over.

She kept fingering the necklace all through their supper at the Ground Six Restaurant. They were on the top floor of the Relax Inn Hotel and through the window, beside their table, she could see the lights of the boats twinkling in the harbour. From another window she caught a glimpse of the magnificent Grand Mosque, its golden dome illuminated against the velvet darkness of the sky.

Sipping her coffee, she reflected that the food had been superb. Tim had chosen a selection of spicy side dishes to accompany their special Maldivian curry, and her tongue was still tingling from the delicious tastes she'd experienced.

'It's been a wonderful end to a fantastic day,' she said, reaching across the table to touch Tim's hand.

Almost immediately, she moved it back again. They might have been lovers today but she didn't want Tim to think she was going to become over-familiar or proprietorial in public.

He smiled. 'The day isn't finished yet. You don't have to go back to Kamafaroo tonight. We could stay here. I'll get a room with a view of the harbour and you can go back in the morning. The boat crew won't mind if I give them a good tip. They're always happy to have a night out in Male, before sleeping on the boat.'

All the time Tim had been speaking she'd been wrestling with her own thoughts, but she'd forced herself to come to a sober, rational decision.

'No, I've got to go,' she said in a firm voice that was as much to convince herself as Tim.

He leaned back in his chair, a wry smile on his face. 'Declaring your independence again, are you?'

She smiled. 'Something like that.'

How could she tell him that if he made love to her again tonight, all her resolutions would be hopelessly weakened?

He walked back through the evening crowds to the boat with her, his hand almost but not quite touching hers.

'Thanks for a wonderful day,' she said, as she climbed on board.

The crew were watching. He didn't kiss her. She told herself she was glad. Their relationship was a secret, private affair and the fewer people who knew about it the better. It would be much simpler when the inevitable split occurred.

The engines revved and the boat skimmed across the water. Tim was watching from the harbourside. He waved as the boat moved behind a large tanker, obscuring him from her view.

For a flickering moment she wondered who Tim would spoil on Valentine's Day next year, before banishing the treacherous thought from her mind.

Where Tim was concerned, she must live in the present and enjoy every precious moment.

CHAPTER SEVEN

KATIE'S desk calendar confirmed that it had been three weeks since she'd seen Tim, three whole weeks since Valentine's Day! As Katie thumbed through the pile of case notes that Nurse Sabia had just given her, she told herself that it was going to be a busy morning so she must concentrate and stop thinking about Tim.

She took a sip of the coffee which Nurse Sabia had supplied along with the case notes and leaned back in her chair. Maybe she could indulge herself for a couple of minutes. It wasn't yet nine o'clock and she was getting into the swing of Maldivian time.

In London everyone was obsessed by the clock, but here on Kamafaroo the sun rose in the morning, set in the evening and in between you did what had to be done at a leisurely pace so that the heat didn't deplete your store of energy.

She felt her store was decidedly depleted today, having spent a very restless night, tossing and turning, changing from air conditioning to fan and vice versa to no effect. In fact, she hadn't slept well for three weeks.

He could have phoned!

He'd phoned on that first morning, the morning after her idyllic Valentine's Day birthday, to remind her that he was going to a medical conference in New Delhi at the end of the week. She remembered he'd mentioned it that night they'd had the discussion with Rick. Dr Afraz would be in charge if she had any problems she couldn't handle.

140

He'd sounded sort of...strained? As if somebody was with him in his room? As if he regretted coming on so strong the day before?

She remembered how she'd been holding back, not wanting to ask how long he'd be away. Later, when she'd spoken to Dr Afraz, she'd learned that the conference would last two weeks.

Nurse Sabia poked her head round the door, her long dark plait swinging over her shoulder and a bright, friendly, fresh-as-a-daisy, morning-after-a-good-night's-sleep type of smile.

'Are you ready for the first patient, Dr Mandrake?'

'Yes, yes,' she said quickly, forcing herself to give all her attention to her work.

She opened the first case notes. Thadheeja—what a pretty first name! The second name, the family name, was something unpronounceable.

'Do bring Thadheeja in, Nurse Sabia.'

It was Musa's mother. Katie recognised her as soon as she stepped through the door, even though the name on the case file hadn't meant anything to her. She smiled reassuringly at the small, many-layered, sari-enshrouded figure and stood up to welcome her.

Remembering her patient's limited English, she asked Nurse Sabia to stay and help with the language problem.

'Do sit down, Thadheeja,' Katie said gently, drawing out the chair at the side of her desk.

As her patient pulled aside the layers of coloured robes to enable her to sit, it was obvious to Katie that she was pregnant. She hadn't noticed the pregnancy on the couple of times she'd briefly met Thadheeja, once when she'd brought Musa in to have his leg stitched and once in the village when they'd asked Musa to stop selling water.

It was understandable she might not have noticed it. Enshrouded in layers of cloth, the women from the village had no need of maternity wear.

When Thadheeja was comfortably settled on the chair Katie began, carefully, to ask questions about the pregnancy. With the help of Nurse Sabia, she discovered that Musa's mother had been experiencing back pain during the night.

It was impossible to ascertain how far advanced the pregnancy was because Thadheeja had no idea about dates so Katie settled her patient on the examination couch.

'How is Musa?' she asked, as she pulled on a pair of sterile gloves.

The mother's eyes brightened. 'Good. Musa school.'

Katie leaned over her patient. 'I'm glad he's at school. Does Musa like going to school?'

Nurse Sabia translated and, from the torrent of conversation that ensued, Katie gathered that Musa was thrilled to be a pupil at last. In fact, it sounded as if he was already top of the class and well on the way to running the establishment!

'Musa has told his mother he wants to be a doctor,' Nurse Sabia told Katie.

Katie paused in her examination of Thadheeja's well-rounded abdomen. 'I wonder why.'

'Musa want to be like doctor,' Thadheeja said unexpectedly. 'Good man doctor.'

'Oh, you mean Dr Fielding. Yes, he's a very good doctor,' Katie said, placing her ear to the Pinard's foetal stethoscope, the trumpet-shaped instrument which she pressed against the patient's abdomen so that she could listen to the baby's heartbeat.

Turning her head on one side, she narrowed her eyes

as she tried to cut out all extraneous sounds. The baby's heartbeat was regular and strong but the pregnancy was well advanced and the mother hadn't had any antenatal treatment.

A movement by the door distracted her attention from her patient. Her eyes widened with disbelief. Well, talk of the devil! She hadn't heard the door open but the 'good man doctor' had suddenly materialised. She felt the blood rush to her face as she straightened.

'Good morning, Dr Fielding. I didn't know you were back from your conference.'

There was a wry smile on Tim's face. 'Good morning, Dr Mandrake, Nurse Sabia.' He nodded in her direction.

'Nurse Sabia is helping me to translate for Thadheeja, Musa's mother.'

'You've got some patients waiting to register outside in the reception area, Nurse Sabia,' Tim said. 'I can help with translation.'

He walked to the other side of the examination couch and leaned over to say something which made their patient smile. Katie was intrigued by the instant rapport between them.

'What did you say?' she asked.

'Loosely translated, I said she'd been a dark horse, keeping this pregnancy quiet.' He lowered his voice. 'No point in talking about the importance of regular antenatal care at this late stage. What made her come in today?'

'She had back pains in the night. The baby's heartbeat is strong and the uterus isn't contracting so...'

'Have you done an internal examination yet?'

'I was just about to when you sprang in from outer space.'

His eyes flickered at her abrasive tone. 'Meaning?'

'Meaning you could have phoned. They do have phones in New Delhi, I presume.'

As soon as she'd said it she regretted it. All her pent-up frustration had surfaced, but she shouldn't have berated him as if he owed her an explanation. Theirs was a no-strings relationship and the last thing Tim needed was a possessive woman.

'Shall we talk about this later?' he said evenly. 'Perhaps you'd like to do the internal examination and then we can discuss the case in more detail.'

He gave an encouraging smile to Musa's mother, followed by a few words in her language, before going out into the reception area.

It seemed obvious to Katie that he was having second thoughts. He'd got carried away on Valentine's Day and now he was drawing back from her, trying to re-establish the professional relationship they'd had previously.

She deliberately pushed him from her mind, knowing she had to give one hundred per cent to this patient and her precious unborn baby.

Her internal examination revealed that the birth canal was in good condition. There was no dilation at the top of the birth canal so the back pain Thadheeja had been experiencing hadn't been labour pains. It was probably due to the mechanical stresses imposed on the mother's pelvis during the latter stages of pregnancy and would disappear after the baby was born.

The baby was settling low in the womb, and from the size of it she estimated that the birth would be some time within the next month.

Tim came back just as Katie was washing her hands. She glanced up and saw that he was his usual confident self. It was as if they were simply professional colleagues again. Fine! If that was what he wanted, that was how she'd play it too.

Her mind fully focussed on the patient's pregnancy, she began to discuss the findings of her examination with Tim.

'With no contractions of the uterus and no dilation of the cervix we have to assume that the back pain isn't indicating an imminent delivery,' Tim said.

Katie nodded. 'The increased laxity of the joints in the spine, which is normal in pregnancy, sometimes causes pain. She probably did too much work or lifted something heavy. She's not very robust.'

Tim smiled at Thadheeja, who was now sitting up on the couch, gathering her layers around her.

He continued to smile reassuringly as he spoke slowly and carefully in her language.

'I've asked Thadheeja to come to the hospital every day until the baby is born,' he told Katie. 'Nurse Sabia can arrange some of the antenatal tests this morning. I'm going to prescribe a course of iron and folic acid tablets to start off with.'

He pressed the intercom button and asked Nurse Sabia to take Thadheeja to the obstetrics unit so that Sister Habaid could start her on a course of antenatal treatment. Then he explained to Thadheeja what was going to happen, before taking her to the door.

Katie gathered that Tim was reassuring her that she could go home to her family when she'd been to see Sister Habaid. Through the open door she watched him hand over the case notes, before entrusting his patient to the capable Nurse Sabia.

He was coming back. She took a deep breath to calm herself as she got on with clearing up the examination area.

He closed the door and turned back towards her. Her heart missed a beat as he strode purposefully, across the room. She dropped the Pinard's stethoscope in mid-clean. It landed with a clatter on the top layer of the examination trolley.

He was reaching out towards her, his strong arms encircling her.

'I've missed you so much, Katie,' he said before his lips covered hers in a long, tender kiss that nearly took her breath away.

She felt her emotions go into a flat spin. So he wasn't going to play the standoffish boss after all!

He pulled himself away and held her at arm's length. 'Let me have a look at you. Mmm, you're just as I remember. A little tired, perhaps? Have you been working too hard?'

'No more than usual.'

She wasn't going to tell him about the sleepless nights.

He ran a hand through his dark hair, scraping back the strands that fell over his eyes. She could see his expression now—warm, convincingly tender. Maybe he really had missed her! Her misgivings were beginning to evaporate.

He gestured towards the reception area. 'You've got a crowd of people out there, waiting to see you, so I'll give you a hand. Let me take some of those case notes and I'll set myself up in the room next door.'

He paused and gave her a broad smile that tugged at her heartstrings. 'When we've finished we could have lunch together.'

'That would be nice.'

She was deliberately holding back now. Maybe she should have told him she was too busy, but his kiss had set her senses on fire again, although she was bound to admit that this see-sawing of her emotions was exhausting. Did he think he could leave her for three weeks without a word and then take up where he'd left off? Were these going to be the rules of their game?

She swallowed hard as she faced him, taking in his tanned, handsome face, his long, muscular, chino-clad legs, the well-pressed cotton shirt, open at the neck to reveal part of the rugged chest she'd snuggled against...

She came to a decision. If this was all she could hope for, she'd go along with it for as long as it lasted. Because it was probably only once in a lifetime you felt like this about somebody.

She didn't resist when he pulled her gently against him.

'If I seemed distant when I first arrived it was because I don't want the medical grapevine to buzz with rumours about us. I know you wouldn't want that either, would you?'

'Of course not!'

She stared up into his deep blue eyes, her own eyes unflickering and intent on convincing him that she agreed entirely that their transient relationship should be kept secret.

'In the dining room at lunchtime,' she began, 'we must be careful to—'

'Who said anything about the dining room?'

He was smiling down at her with a heart-rending expression in his eyes. Her legs felt limp; desire was welling up inside her. If he was going to suggest room service at her bungalow the temptation would be impossible to resist.

Maybe she should put up some resistance, just to show him he couldn't have it all his own way!

'Tim…'

'I've hired a small speedboat for the afternoon.'

'But—'

'I've ordered a picnic lunch. The two boys who'll crew the boat have no connection with the medical service so we'll be totally unobserved on our desert island.'

'Which desert island?' she managed to ask, as she tried to calm her fluttering heart.

He laughed. 'Does it matter? There are so many uninhabited islands round here. The one I have in mind has a fiendishly difficult, long name. Sounds like Fishybarbecue or something like that, which is exactly what we'll have for lunch.'

She was laughing with him now. It was impossible to resist this man, even though she was still hopping mad because he hadn't phoned.

A warning bell was sounding at the back of her mind. Don't get too involved. Remember how you felt when Rick let you down.

But Tim wouldn't be able to let her down if she didn't expect anything from him…like phone calls when he went away. If she wasn't committed to him he couldn't hurt her. Easier said than done, she thought wryly as she turned away to rearrange the pile of case notes.

'You take these, Tim. They're all first visits. I've kept the repeat visits because these patients will expect to see me. It's more reassuring for them.'

He put a finger under her chin and tilted her face. Gently, he kissed the tip of her nose.

'Don't work too hard. I may need some help in catching the lunch.'

There was a quiet tap on the door and Nurse Sabia came in. They sprang apart but Katie was sure they hadn't fooled the observant young woman. She didn't

mind any more. It was Tim who was hell-bent on holding onto his professional reputation. Wouldn't do to have
people think he seduced all the medical staff who came
out here for a brief spell of duty.

Mustn't get bitter! This was what they'd agreed from
the outset. Tim was only sticking to the rules they'd set.
She was the one who wanted to change them.

'There's a patient who needs to be seen at once,'
Nurse Sabia said quickly. 'She slipped on one of the
rocks and her left arm is very painful.'

'Bring her in, Nurse,' Tim said. 'We'll examine her
in here.'

It was obvious that their small, plump, middle-aged
patient was in considerable pain as she walked into the
room, leaning heavily on a tall, worried-looking, grey-
haired man who started to explain. 'Jane had just finished swimming. She was clambering over the rocks
and... I'm Jane's husband, Gordon Coombes.'

'Do sit down, Mr Coombes, while we take a look at
your wife,' Katie said. 'Mrs Coombes, if you'd like to
swallow these tablets they should take the edge off the
pain.'

'Thanks, Doctor.'

Jane Coombes gave a brave smile as she accepted a
glass of water from Tim to chase down the painkillers.

Katie put pillows against her patient's back as she
settled her on the examination trolley. Gently she eased
the arm out of the makeshift sling.

'It's the tablecloth from my room,' Mrs Coombes
said. 'It was the first thing that— Ow!'

Tim had placed his experienced fingers gently on the
swollen area of the forearm.

'I think you've broken the ulna,' he said in a quiet,
sympathetic tone to their patient. 'The ulna is one of the

two long bones in the forearm. We'll take an X-ray to confirm this and then we'll set it in plaster of Paris.'

Katie called through to Nurse Sabia, asking her to apologise to the other patients who would be kept waiting while they took their patient in a wheelchair to the small X-ray room.

There was no doubt about the diagnosis when they held the plates against the illuminated screen. The X-rays of the forearm revealed a transverse break of the ulna, as Tim had suspected.

In the little plaster room, next door to the X-ray room, Katie soaked the plaster bandages in water, handing them over to Tim who was holding the arm and hand in position with the wrist slightly tilted and the thumb pointing upwards. When the bandages had been fixed around the arm, Katie smoothed down the already setting plaster with her fingers.

'How long will I have to keep the plaster on?' Mrs Coombes asked in a resigned tone.

'Five to six weeks,' Katie said. 'We'll give you the X-rays to show to your doctor back in the UK. I'll give you some painkillers to take while you're still out here in the Maldives and for the journey home.'

Jane Coombes pulled a wry face. 'We came out here to celebrate our fortieth wedding anniversary, Doctor.'

'Congratulations on the anniversary!' Katie said. 'But I'm sorry this had to happen.'

Back in the surgery Mr Coombes leaned forward and patted his wife's good arm. 'Don't worry, dear. I'll look after you. It could have been worse. It might have been your leg.'

As Katie watched the grey-haired man help his wife from the room she reflected that this mature couple had a special kind of love. Theirs appeared to be a serene, undemanding relationship.

As she looked across at Tim, who was flicking through the case notes she'd given him, she reflected that there was something beyond the heady, all-consuming passion they'd experienced on Valentine's Day. But without commitment they would never experience it.

She watched him going out, his step jaunty and assured—a very independent man, happy to remain footloose and fancy-free.

She gave a deep sigh as she opened the next case file and pressed the intercom button. Who would have thought she would ever want to involve herself with a man again after all she'd suffered with Rick?

She must be mad even to contemplate it! In the first place, Tim was fiercely independent—he'd had his fingers burned once and he wasn't going to risk a repeat of the painful experience. Second, so had she, and she ought to recognise that the idea would kill the lighthearted, fun-filled relationship that was building up between them.

So make sure you keep your emotional distance, girl!

She threw herself wholeheartedly into her work for the rest of the morning. The medical problems were routine and, with Tim's help, all the patients were seen by midday.

A young couple had been suffering from upset stomachs but Katie diagnosed this as being due to overindulgence at the bar and prescribed some medicine to calm and soothe the digestive system. She also advised a couple of alcohol-free days but, from the looks on their faces, she doubted if her advice would be taken!

'Well, they are on holiday,' she told Tim later. 'If they choose to abuse their bodies they'll just have to accept the consequences.'

'Exactly! Now, that's enough shop talk.'

They were walking down to the landing stage where Katie could see a rather swish speedboat waiting for them.

'I hope I've packed the right things. What do you pack for an afternoon on a desert island?'

He gave her a rakish grin. 'Theoretically nothing! We've got the sun, the sea, each other...'

Oh, the smoothy! She reviewed the contents of her bag. A couple of bikinis, high factor sun lotion—but maybe they'd be sheltering under the palm trees. Her pulses started racing so she stopped anticipating the afternoon ahead. Let the wheel turn and see what happened.

Tim put out a hand to help her into the boat. She could see several baskets stowed through in the cabin.

'Is that our lunch?'

He smiled. 'We've got everything with us except the main ingredient, the fish.'

He gestured over the water with a wide sweep of his arm.

'We'll pick up the main course when we get away from the shore.'

'I've never fished before,' she said in a loud voice to make herself heard above the noise of the engines, which were starting up.

'This is a beginner's paradise,' he shouted. 'You just drop a line with some bait over the side and they come nibbling.'

It was quite true. When the two-man crew cut the engines it was a simple matter to ensnare the fish. Within minutes Tim had caught a superb kingfish. Then Katie, feeling a tugging at her line, hauled in another one and laughed with excitement.

'That's more than enough for our lunch, Tim,' she told him as he handed over the fish to the crew.

'I'm glad I don't have to deal with the preparation,' she said, when Tim returned to his seat beside her at the back of the boat. 'I love eating fish but I hate to think of—'

'They don't suffer,' Tim told her quickly. 'I used to be squeamish like that when I was a child but my father soon taught me to be objective about it. Think of it as a natural cycle. Big fish eat little fish and then we come along and eat the big fish. Don't worry, the crew will have seen to them by now.'

She nodded. That was the first time Tim had spoken about his father in such a matter-of-fact tone.

She leaned back against the side of the boat, closing her eyes after she had looked through her sunglasses at the clear blue expanse above her head. Not a cloud in the sky. All around her the sea was perfectly calm, but the boat was carving a wide swathe through it, churning up the water and creating a cooling spray.

They were approaching a group of small islands. She smoothed back her fly-away hair, trying to secure it into the black velvet band that was supposed to keep it under control.

Calmly, Tim took hold of both her hands and unloosened her hair. 'Leave it like that—it looks fabulous!'

He was snapping away with his camera focussed on her.

'You won't get anything but hair,' she said with a laugh.

'Yes, I will. Turn your head so that the airstream is

against your face. That's it...perfect! That's the shot I want to remember you by.'

She swallowed hard. That was the photo he would take out of a drawer in years to come and chuck in the bin, wondering who on earth the woman with the unruly hair was.

She turned away and looked towards the shoreline of the island they were approaching. She told herself she mustn't allow thoughts of the future to spoil her time with Tim. She must live in the present, enjoy each moment they were together.

She raised her hand and pointed. 'It looks like a real Robinson Crusoe island. Is it really uninhabited?'

He laughed. 'It is, until we arrive. Shall we take possession?'

CHAPTER EIGHT

'IT'S beautiful!' As Katie ran up the beach from the boat she could smell the scent of the wild frangipani that grew on the edge of the sand. Having changed into her bikini on the boat, she felt delightfully free of all the trappings of civilisation.

She was aware that Tim, who'd been giving instructions to the crew about where to set up the barbecue, was running up behind her. Suddenly she felt his arms encircle her waist and she was lifted off her feet.

'Our own paradise on earth! Not another soul in sight,' he said, setting her down again on the warm sand.

She wriggled her toes in the sand. In the shade of the palm trees, where they'd now arrived, it was still possible to walk barefoot even with the strong afternoon sun beating down on the broad leaves.

'Not another soul except the crew, toiling over our lunch,' she said prosaically.

'We've done our toiling for the day,' he told her with a grin. 'Now's the time for relaxation.'

He sank into the warm sand, one arm pulling her with him. He was wearing only his swimming trunks. The feel of his skin against hers was decidedly unnerving.

She pulled away and jumped to her feet. 'Come on, lazybones! I want to explore.'

She ignored the surprised—or hurt—expression in his eyes as she turned away and made for a natural path through the thick foliage.

'Why don't you explore by yourself?' he called.

She turned in dismay but he was already scrambling to his feet, a teasing smile on his face.

'Only joking! I wouldn't let you walk alone through that stretch of jungle. You might get eaten by a tiger or something.'

His hand was almost touching hers. She took hold of it, comforted by the strength of his grasp.

'What sort of creatures live on a desert island like this?'

He smiled as he put out his hand to move a few wayward strands of hair that were falling over her eyes. The movement felt like a semi-caress, or was he trying to be proprietorial? She realised with a pang of intense emotion that, either way, she didn't mind. It was hopeless to try and curb her feelings!

'No tigers, of course,' he told her. 'The snakes have a dangerous bite if you disturb them, and the ants will sting you if you sit near them. The birds are friendly but you have to watch out for the monkeys. Look, there's a family of them up in that tree!'

She stopped walking along the narrow path and looked upwards, fascinated to watch the antics of the chattering monkeys.

She laughed. 'They're behaving like excitable children at a play group. I didn't know they were dangerous.'

'They're not, unless you provoke them. The only threat that monkeys pose is when they steal your lunch. They'll eat anything. They've even learned how to bite open those packets of fruit juice you can buy because this is a favourite spot for visiting tourists.'

She moved ahead of him on the narrow path. 'Then you haven't got exclusive rights to this island, Mr Crusoe?'

'Afraid not, Miss Friday. But I'm keeping a weather eye open for the marauding pirates.'

It wasn't a very big island. In a very short time they'd walked across to the other side and then back via the beach to the place where the boat was moored.

Katie was delighted by what she saw. 'Wow! They've really set up camp here!'

While they'd been exploring, the crew had cleared the pebbles from a small section of beach and lit a fire in a split oil drum. A metal rack over the top held the fish they'd caught.

She sat down under a large, multicoloured umbrella which shaded a wooden table on which she saw a bowl of salad, some bread rolls and an ice bucket containing a bottle of white wine.

Tim joined her, tilting the umbrella to get maximum shade. He opened the wine with the conveniently placed corkscrew and poured out a couple of glasses.

The two young crew members brought the fish across from the barbecue on a large serving dish, their faces wreathed in smiles as they presented it.

'Thanks very much. That looks wonderful!' Tim said. 'Are you going to join us?'

The young men shook their heads but agreed to take some of the fish back to the boat where they were going to eat their lunch.

'I don't think I've ever tasted fish like this before, but I couldn't finish it all,' Katie said, as she put down her knife and fork.

'It's the fresh delivery that makes it taste so good.' Tim reached across and topped up her glass. 'Would you like some fruit?'

She chose an orange from the basket on the table and began to remove the peel. Now that the crew were out of sight in the cabin of the boat she realised that they really were alone. Looking across the table, she saw that Tim was watching her with a fond expression.

'I missed you a lot while I was away,' he said quietly.

She put the orange on her plate, wiping her hands on the large cotton napkin.

'I missed you too. I thought…I mean, I expected you would phone.'

'Did you?' He looked genuinely surprised.

'Well, of course I did!' She realised she was being too forceful so she mellowed her tone. 'What I meant to say was, after the day we'd spent together I—'

She broke off, knowing that she mustn't tell him she hoped it had meant something to him. Mustn't become possessive.

'I know what you're trying to say, Katie.'

Her eyebrows shot upwards. 'Do you?'

'After you'd gone back to Kamafaroo on Valentine's Day I realised you were quite right not to stay the night. We both needed space to think out where we were going together. I was asking too much of you.'

'No! It was a wonderful day! I—'

'I enjoyed it too. But I remembered how adamant you were when you first came out that you didn't want a serious relationship ever again. I could see that in bringing you together with Rick to extract some explanations from him I'd helped you, but coming on as strong as I did was enough to frighten you away. And I really value your friendship, Katie.'

She swallowed hard. Friendship! Was that all she meant to him?

'So that's why I didn't phone,' he said evenly. 'I wanted to give you time to recover. And I wanted time to sort out my own feelings.'

She stared at him, hardly daring to hope after what he'd just said.

'I was disturbed by the depth of my feelings for you,' he said carefully. 'I'd hoped to stay neutral...and I'm still trying but...'

He stood up and came round the table. She also rose and he took her in his arms. He held her close and murmured into her hair. 'I don't want anything to change between us. If we have to start making plans about our future it will spoil everything.'

She lifted her head so that her lips were brushing against his as she spoke. The feeling of relief was so strong that she could have cried. He really did care for her. All he was afraid of was commitment. She could live with that if it meant they could go on seeing each other. 'No plans, no commitment,' she whispered. 'Just you and me together for as long as it lasts.'

He kissed her hungrily, his lips hard against hers. She gave a low moan of desire and he scooped her up in his arms, carrying her effortlessly up the beach into the seclusion and deep shade of the palm trees.

Swimwear was tossed into a pile on the sand as they reached out for each other. She clung to him, revelling in each caress of his sensual fingers as he explored her body, sending shivers of longing deep inside her. She strained against him, her heart pounding madly as he entered her. And when the ultimate, delirious climax came she cried out, barely able to sustain the waves of ecstasy that flooded through her.

A muffled thud awakened her. She opened her eyes to see a coconut had fallen from a tree and cracked open in the sand near her feet. She curled her feet underneath her and looked at Tim whose face was only inches from

hers. He was still asleep, his breathing steady and rhythmic. He looked as if he was dreaming, his eyes making
rapid movements beneath their lids.

Was he dreaming about her? About their exquisite
love-making? She rolled over on her back and looked
up at the canopy of palm leaves.

This fantastic feeling of rapport that they had between
them was going to be enough, wasn't it? She mustn't
ask for more. She must go along with their so-called
friendship for as long as it lasted, which would probably
be when she went back to the UK in June.

No strings, no demands...

Tim was stirring in his sleep. He opened his eyes and
looked directly at her. Instantly, his arms reached out for
her.

'Come here,' he said huskily, pulling her against him.

His kiss was gentle, the kiss of a satisfied lover. She
moved in his arms, the dampness of their hot skins making them stick to each other.

She pulled herself away and stood up. 'I'm going for
a swim.'

Their section of the beach was out of sight of the boat.
She ran naked into the sea. Tim was close behind her.
They swam together, side by side, in the calm, warm
water.

Neither of them spoke of the ecstatic experience
they'd enjoyed together. It was as if words would have
broken the magic spell. After the swim they ran, hand
in hand, along the beach until the sun had dried their
bodies.

'Back to civilisation!' Tim said, as they put on their
discarded swimwear in the shade of the palm trees.

Katie looked down at the hollow in the sand which
had been their cosy little love nest for the afternoon.

'Yes, back to reality,' she said.

He caught her in his arms. 'It's been another wonderful day. And this time I'm not worried about you. We understand each other again.'

'Absolutely!' she said, with as much conviction as she could muster. 'Race you back to the boat.'

Nurse Sabia came to meet them as soon as they went in through the door of the hospital.

'Thank goodness you're back! Thadheeja has just come back into hospital again. She's complaining of headaches now and her blood pressure is dangerously high. Look, here's the chart I've made out for her. You can see...'

Katie could see they had an emergency on their hands. Headache coupled with such high blood pressure could be indicative of pre-eclampsia, the medical condition that warned that full eclampsia might follow. And patients who went into a state of full eclampsia sometimes died.

She looked up at Tim and saw her own worried thoughts mirrored in his eyes.

'Where is she?'

'In Obstetrics,' Nurse Sabia said. 'Sister Habaid has...'

They were already out of earshot, hurrying down the corridor.

They found their patient in a small room at the side of the main ward. Sister Habaid was bending over her. She looked up with an expression of relief.

Katie was impressed by how quickly Tim could transform himself from carefree lover with sand between his toes to caring doctor. He assessed the situation rapidly after a brief but comprehensive examination of their patient. There were more tests which could be done to confirm their diagnosis but it would be dangerous to delay treatment.

Tim drew Katie on one side and they conferred.

'We'll have to induce or do a Caesarean section,' he said quickly. 'The baby is suffering distress and Thadheeja's life is in danger. We've got to deliver the baby as soon as possible.'

Katie nodded. 'I agree. So? Caesarean or...?'

'A Caesarean would be safer.'

She felt relieved. 'That's what I would advise. I couldn't bear it if anything happened to Musa's mother.'

He raised an eyebrow. 'Let's try to remain objective. All our patients are important. We don't have favourites.'

She gave a bleak smile. 'But if we did...'

'If we did, Thadheeja would be head of the queue,' he put in wryly. 'Will you prepare the patient, Doctor, while I investigate the operating theatre? It worked well for our appendicectomy. Let's hope...'

She didn't hear what Tim was hoping because he'd already shot off outside the side ward. As she turned to watch him go she noticed a small, dark face peeping round the door.

'Musa!'

The little boy advanced into the room. 'I brought my mother's supper,' he said proudly, swinging the small cooking pot. 'I made it myself. Her favourite.'

He was moving towards the bed but Katie could see that Thadheeja was in no mood for a visit, even from her beloved son who was going to become a doctor.

Katie caught Musa by the shoulders. 'Your mother is going to have a little sleep. Let me take her supper and keep it until she wakes up.'

Musa frowned as he looked up at Katie. 'Is she going to have the baby now? Shall I bring my grandmother and my aunt to—?'

'Soon you can bring them,' Katie said quickly. 'Who is in charge of your little brothers?'

Musa drew himself to his full height. 'I am. My father is working on a big ship for many weeks.'

'Well, perhaps you'd like to go back and see that they're all right. Call your grandmother and aunt to help you.'

She took his hand and walked with him to the door.

From the bed, Thadheeja gave an involuntary gasp of pain. On her way back, Katie reached for the syringe and drew up the premedication. Her patient was going to need a general anaesthetic.

Tim was talking quietly to Thadheeja as she lay in her bed in a drowsy post-operative state.

Katie could tell from her limited knowledge of the local language and also from the smile on Thadheeja's face that he was passing on the good news to their exhausted but happy patient that she had a beautiful, healthy little daughter.

'With three young sons at home, Thadheeja says it is a miracle to have produced a daughter,' Tim said. 'She is asking if she can call it Katie because she says you have been so good to her.'

'Of course. I'll be delighted.'

She leaned across and patted her patient's hand. So far they had found it difficult to remove the baby from its mother. Ever since she had come round from the anaesthetic she had clung to her precious bundle of joy.

'Thadheeja told me she thinks going to sleep and waking up with the baby is the best form of childbirth,' Tim said quietly. 'She's actually asked me to make sure we can both be there for her next baby and deliver it in this magical way.'

'Well, maybe you can, but I'm not sure where I'll be,' she said evenly.

His eyes flickered. 'When is it you're due to go back to the UK?'

She swallowed hard. 'June.'

'Did my mother like her supper?' said a little voice.

Katie smiled down at the small boy who had crept in, unobserved.

'She's been asleep, Musa, and while she was asleep we were able to deliver her baby. You've got a little sister.'

Musa's brown eyes widened in surprise. 'A sister? I thought it would be another brother.'

Thadheeja called to him from the bed. The hand that wasn't holding the baby reached out towards him. He ran to his mother and as he peeped at the tiny bundle in her arms his little face lit up with pleasure. Settling himself on the chair beside the bed, he leaned against his mother and she held him close to her.

Katie felt a lump rise in her throat as she looked at mother, son and precious baby daughter.

'I'm glad we got back in time,' she whispered to Tim.

There was the sound of voices out in the corridor. Through the open door came Musa's grandmother, aunt and his two little brothers.

They were all smiles as they gathered round the bed, chattering excitedly as they admired the baby girl.

'Don't you think Thadheeja should get some rest?' Katie said to Tim.

He gave her a wry smile. 'The women of the family are an essential part of postnatal care. They'll look after

Thadheeja now. If she feels sleepy she'll sleep, regardless of whether she has visitors or not. Maldivians don't stand on ceremony.'

'Talking of sleep, I'm going to take myself off to bed,' Katie said quietly.

Tim's eyes flickered. 'So am I. I need to get back to Male,' he added quickly.

'Of course.'

This was how it would be until she went back to the UK. Working together, side by side, coupled with some idyllic off-duty interludes. That was going to be enough, wasn't it?

CHAPTER NINE

TIME was passing too quickly. Throughout March and April Katie had told herself that she still had plenty of time to enjoy her life on Kamafaroo. She wouldn't think about having to leave in June. But now that it was May, and she had only a few weeks to go, a sense of urgency was setting in.

As she sat at her desk, leafing through the case notes before her morning surgery, she began wondering if the medical board had appointed her successor yet. She would ask Tim when he came in this morning.

About a month ago she'd had to show a potential candidate around the hospital. This tall, attractive woman, looking far too young to be a doctor, had arrived in Reception one day, explaining that she was spending a week's holiday on the island before deciding whether or not to apply for the post which had been advertised in one of the medical journals. Interviews were to take place in London.

With a sinking feeling, Katie made a mental note to ask Tim if he'd heard anything about her replacement.

Thinking about Tim made her reflect that for the past few weeks their lives had fallen into a set pattern. They worked well together in hospital and they enjoyed their off-duty time together. She couldn't bear to think of giving all this up! There must be a way to make Tim realise that they should...

No! She checked herself even before the tantalising idea of a more permanent relationship with Tim could surface again. He'd made it abundantly clear that they were simply to enjoy each moment together. Commitment would change everything.

She knew it was Tim arriving when she heard the strong, sure footsteps approaching her door. He knocked, but came in almost immediately. So sure of himself! So sure that she would welcome him! Which she always did.

As she watched him stride across the room she wondered, fleetingly, if she should have held back more. If she'd played hard to get, would Tim now have been begging her to stay on with him?

She doubted it! His problem with commitment hadn't changed since that wretched woman, Rebecca, had let him down. And there wasn't a thing she could do about that.

'Good morning, Dr Mandrake.' His lips brushed the side of her cheek.

'Good morning, Dr Fielding.'

She could smell his distinctive aftershave, and the memories it evoked were playing havoc with her efforts to put herself in a working mood.

He leaned against her desk. 'I've just had an early morning dive with Rick over on Fanassi.'

'How nice!'

The sarcasm in her voice belied her words. Familiar waves of resentment erupted inside her when she thought of Rick, and for a brief moment she understood once more why Tim found it difficult to forgive or forget the profoundly disturbing, two-timing Rebecca.

He put a hand over hers. 'Give the poor chap a chance, Katie.' He paused. 'He wants to see you again.'

She frowned. 'Why? I'd much prefer to try and forget he exists.'

'I'm sure you would, but Rick says he has something important to tell you. Will you come with me to see him this afternoon?'

She began to weaken when she heard his pleading tone. If Tim was with her she could survive the ordeal.

'I can't imagine what he wants to tell me, but...OK. But don't leave me alone with him, will you?'

'Of course not.' He stood up. 'What's that noise in Reception?'

'Sounds like someone's having an argument with Nurse Sabia. Perhaps I'd better—'

The door burst open. A harassed-looking blonde-haired woman, carrying a child, came in, followed by an apologetic Nurse Sabia in hot pursuit.

'I'm sorry, Dr Mandrake, but this lady insisted on seeing you, without being registered. I told her that—'

'That's OK, Nurse Sabia,' Katie said. 'She can be registered later.'

She asked the distraught woman to sit down. The fractious child started to cry. Tim reached down and lifted her from her mother's lap.

'What's your little girl's name?' he asked, producing a small teddy bear from the top of the cupboard.

The child stopped crying and clutched at the bear, poking an exploratory finger around the plastic eyes.

'She's called Vanessa,' the mother said. 'And I think she's got measles.'

'Let's hope not,' Tim said evenly. 'The native people of the Maldives have never suffered from the infectious diseases we get in the West so they have no immunity to them. If Vanessa has measles she'll have to go back home.'

'But we're on holiday!' the mother said warily. 'We only just arrived a couple of days ago.'

'Let's take a look, shall we?' Katie said quickly, as she followed Tim over to the examination couch. 'How old is Vanessa, Mrs...?

'Mrs Gardiner. Call me Pam. Vanessa's nearly six. She must have caught the measles at school before we left.'

'Hasn't Vanessa been immunised against measles?'

Vanessa's mum looked sheepish. 'Well, no. Her dad and I talked it over and decided we'd rather take a chance. You hear such awful things about immunisation in the paper and on the telly, don't you?'

'Those are the few, usually unproven cases that get blown up out of all proportion,' Tim said evenly. 'Since the immunisation programme was introduced we've avoided the deaths, blindness and ear problems that measles sometimes caused.'

Katie was helping to placate the weepy Vanessa while Tim examined her. Her temperature was very high so she would be feeling pretty awful.

'How long has she had this cough and cold?' Tim asked.

'About four days.'

'So if it's measles we should be seeing some spots.'

He began searching at the margin of the child's hair and behind her ears.

Katie persuaded Vanessa to open her mouth long enough for Tim to shine a light inside so that he could check the inside surface of the cheek.

'Can't see any Koplik's spots,' he said.

'Koplik's spots are white spots which appear in the mouth round about the third day when a child has measles,' Katie explained in answer to the mother's query. 'Vanessa hasn't got any.'

'She's rather well wrapped up for this climate, don't

you think?' Tim said, beginning to remove the child's woollen cardigan.

'I always keep my children well wrapped up when they have a bad cold,' Mrs Gardiner said, leaning forward to persuade young Vanessa to slip the remaining sleeve off. 'She coughed all the way here on the aircraft.'

I bet she did! Katie thought. It would have been much better to have kept this sick child at home.

She watched as gently Tim opened the child's shirt to reveal a white chest covered in pink spots.

'I came here as soon as I saw those spots,' the mother said excitedly. 'I knew she had to be seen by a doctor.'

'They're not the typical measles spots, Pam,' Tim said carefully, 'but in view of the high temperature and heavy cold I'd like to keep Vanessa in the hospital for observation.'

'We'll have to take care of her in a room on her own so that if she is infectious she doesn't infect anyone else,' Katie said quickly. 'I'll call Sister Habaid and ask her to make the arrangements.'

By the end of the morning Katie and Tim had seen all the patients on the list and had dealt with a variety of medical problems, none of them serious. Vanessa had been settled in a room off the children's ward and the nurses had been instructed to wear gowns, masks and gloves when taking care of the child.

Halfway through her lunch in the restaurant Katie put down her knife and fork and looked across the table at Tim. Her spicy chicken was delicious but she wasn't hungry. The awful prospect of meeting Rick again loomed large on the horizon.

'Haven't you any idea what he might want?'

'Who?' Tim's expression was one of complete innocence.

'The dreaded Rick, of course!'

She placed her cotton napkin on the table.

Tim raised one eyebrow. 'I haven't a clue what he wants, but you can't duck out now.'

'I've no intention of ducking out. Come on, let's go.'

'But you haven't finished your chicken!'

'I'm not hungry. Besides, I want to go over there while I'm feeling strong enough to see him. If I leave it much longer...'

'OK, OK!' He stood up and moved round to hold her chair.

'Thanks.'

She smiled up at him, aware that they were a source of speculation in the dining room. She didn't care what people thought about her relationship with Tim. Even Tim seemed to have stopped putting up the pretence that they were just good friends.

As they climbed aboard the speedboat that was to take them across to Fanassi she wondered, fleetingly, what sort of a relationship Tim would have with her successor, but the thought was pure torture.

'Have the interviews for my job finished in London?' she asked as they sped across the water.

He looked surprised. 'I've no idea. Why do you ask?'

'I wondered who they'd decided to appoint, that's all,' she said in a matter-of-fact tone. 'You'll let me know if you hear anything, won't you?'

'Of course.'

A jet of spray hit her in the face and she laughed. Tim mopped at her face with a large white handkerchief.

'Rick won't recognise me with my scrubbed-clean face,' she said. 'I always used to wear make-up in

London but out here there's no point. It melts away in no time.'

'You look better without it,' he said quietly. 'You've got a wonderful tan. It suits you.'

'Thank you. I've used lashings of high factor sun protection cream. If some of my patients had listened to me regarding safe sunbathing they wouldn't have come into hospital looking like lobsters.'

He gave a wry smile. 'The trouble is that sometimes they're only out here for a week and they think they can't get enough of the sun. Unlike us. We can have unlimited sun.'

She swallowed hard. 'Until we go back to the UK.'

He remained silent. As she stared across at the rapidly approaching shoreline she wondered what it would be like to wear layers of clothes again, to put on shoes and—horror of horrors—tights!

'Have you got a job to go to when you get back?'

He sounded concerned. She didn't dare to look at him.

'I'm planning to sign on with a locum agency in London,' she said. 'I'll work with them while I'm looking for a permanent hospital post.'

The crew had cut the boat's engines. They were gliding parallel to the jetty. Two men from the diving school were securing the rope around the low concrete post.

Rick was waiting for them on the jetty. He held out his hand to help Katie step from the boat. She couldn't refuse his helpful gesture. His grasp sent an unpleasant shiver through her body. She removed her hand as soon as her feet touched the jetty and looked around, her eyes searching for Tim. He was right behind her.

She turned back to look at Rick. 'You wanted to see me?'

'Yes. Come up to the diving school. We can't talk here.'

'I haven't much time.'

She was hurrying to keep up with the long strides of the two men.

'Neither have I,' Rick said. 'I've got a diving class in half an hour.'

Relief flooded through her. Her ordeal would be short-lived.

'So, what's this all about, Rick?' she asked, as soon as they were inside the diving school.

He ignored the question. 'Would you like a cold drink?'

'No, thanks,' she said automatically.

'I'd like a mineral water,' Tim said.

She sat on a chair by the open door, trying to quell her impatience while drinks were dispensed. Through the door she could see the wide expanse of blue sea. It was positively inviting her to plunge in and cool herself down. In less than half an hour she and Tim would be speeding back across the water. They would take some time off duty and—

'I've got your money.'

Rick's stark statement broke through her thoughts. He walked across, beer-can in hand, and tossed an envelope into her lap. She stared down at it.

'Well, aren't you going to count it? It's all there in US dollars, which you'll be able to change anywhere in the world.'

He was behaving like the tough guy in one of those old black and white movies. Looking at his nervous posturing, she realised what an effort this was for him. Tough guy turned Mr Nice Guy.

'I'm sorry I borrowed it, without asking you,' she

heard him say in a quieter, most un-Rick-like voice, 'but I did try to contact you to explain. Your mother—'

'I know,' she interrupted quickly. 'Since I last saw you, my mother has explained what happened. She was trying to protect me from—'

She broke off as she saw the hurt look in Rick's eyes. All this time she'd been hating him she hadn't realised how vulnerable he was. Nobody could be all bad. Everybody was a mixture of good and bad.

'Your mother was trying to protect you from me, wasn't she?'

'Call it misplaced maternal instinct,' she said evenly. 'Thanks for the money, Rick. I don't know how you managed to save up in such a short time.'

A grin spread over his face as he tapped the side of his nose with his forefinger, and for an instant she saw the man she'd once fallen in love with a long time ago in another life. A bit of a rogue. He hadn't changed, but she had. Especially in what she wanted in a man!

'Ask no questions,' Rick said, his finger still tapping the side of his nose. 'Aren't you going to count it?'

She shook her head. 'I'll take your word.' She stood up.

Rick was holding out his hand. 'Let's shake on it, Katie.'

She braced herself as she held out her hand. 'Goodbye, Rick.' She removed her hand from his grasp.

Outside in the sunlight she realised she was trembling. Tim put his arm round her shoulders and helped her into the boat. She didn't know if Rick was watching and she didn't care.

She leaned against the side of the boat as the engines started up, closing her eyes as she held up her face towards the sun. Mmm…that felt so good!

'That money will come in very useful when you're flat-hunting in London, Katie.'

She opened her eyes and looked at Tim as he sat beside her in the stern of the boat. Why did he have to remind her that the dream was nearly over?

'I hope the money's legal,' she said, putting a hand up to push her hair behind her ears as the boat gathered speed.

His eyes flickered. 'There's something I need to tell you about the money—but not now,' he added quickly.

She leaned towards him, intrigued by his secretive tone.

'You're being very mysterious. Why can't you tell me now?'

'Because it's too complicated to discuss out here on the water, with the boat crew watching us.'

CHAPTER TEN

KATIE followed Tim along the narrow, sandy path that led to Kamafaroo hospital. He'd insisted they checked on their suspected measles case before he answered her questions concerning the money Rick had given her in repayment of his debt. She was desperately trying to quell her curiosity as she took deep breaths of the hot, humid afternoon air.

At the place where the path widened Tim stopped and waited for her to catch up with him.

'If it is measles Vanessa will have to go back to the UK,' he said, as they walked side by side for the final section.

Katie nodded. 'I agree. We can't risk introducing measles to the native population of Kamafaroo and spreading it to the other Maldive islands. It was irresponsible of Pam Gardiner to bring her daughter out in the first place. With a bad cough and cold she should have been kept at home.'

He gave her a wry smile. 'Try telling that to someone who's saved up all year for their two weeks in the sun.'

He pushed open the screen door of the hospital to allow her to walk into the reception area before him.

Nurse Sabia looked up from her desk and smiled.

'How's Vanessa?' Tim asked.

'She's sleeping at the moment. Her mother is with her.'

'We'll go and take a look at her,' Tim said.

Both mother and child were asleep in the side ward.

Pam Gardiner was sitting in the armchair, her head drooping on her chest. She awoke with a start as Tim and Katie walked in.

'Vanessa doesn't seem as hot as she was, Doctor.' The mother leaned across the bed as Tim looked down at her child.

Vanessa stirred and opened her eyes. Seeing Tim, she smiled.

'Where's Teddy?'

Katie picked up the bear off the floor and handed it to the little girl. As she touched the child's hand she could tell that her patient was much cooler. A glance at the chart gave the reassuring information that Vanessa's temperature was only a little above normal.

'Removing all that unnecessary clothing will have helped to lower the temperature,' she said quietly to Tim, as they stood on either side of the bed and peeled back the cotton sheet, before examining their little patient's chest.

'Chest's clearing,' Tim said, as he straightened, after listening with his stethoscope. 'The antibiotics we prescribed are taking effect.'

Katie ran her hand gently over the child's chest. 'These aren't measles spots. They're not developing in crescent-shaped groups. They're not raised, they're too pale and they're too small.'

She looked up at Tim. He was smiling.

'Are you thinking what I'm thinking, Doctor?'

She nodded. 'Prickly heat.'

'Exactly! Thank God it's not measles!'

Pam Gardiner was on her feet again. 'What did you say?'

Tim turned to try and calm the excited mother. 'Vanessa hasn't got measles, Pam. These spots are a simple case of prickly heat, which occurs in a hot climate when the skin is covered up and isn't allowed to breathe properly. The pores get clogged up with perspiration and the skin erupts in tiny spots.'

'What about her cough?'

'The antibiotics should ease that in a few days. It hasn't got anything to do with the prickly heat, of course,' Katie said. 'Pure coincidence.'

Tim folded up his stethoscope and put it back in his bag. 'I would advise you to have Vanessa immunised as soon as you get home.'

'I'm going to, don't worry, Doctor!'

'We'll keep Vanessa in hospital until her temperature is normal again,' he told the relieved mother, 'and then you can have her with you for the rest of your holiday. Bring her back to hospital again if the cough doesn't improve.'

'Make sure the skin is kept dry,' Katie said. 'Frequent bathing in tepid water is a good idea. Pat the skin dry afterwards and apply a light dusting of the special powder I'm prescribing.'

She scribbled on her prescription pad. 'They've got some of this in the dispensary so you could go down and get it. The nurses will show you how to apply it.'

Katie turned to look down at their little patient. 'Take care of Teddy.'

The little girl put up her arms and gave Katie a hug. 'Can I keep him?'

Katie smiled. 'Of course you can. Teddy helped to make you get better, didn't he?'

Her eyes misted over as she glanced briefly around her. How she was going to miss this place! It was going to be such a wrench, leaving everything and everybody—she glanced at Tim—behind.

*　　*　　*

'So, what's all the mystery about Rick's money? Where did he get it from, Tim?'

She decided to come straight to the point as soon as they were alone, sitting together on her veranda. Picking up her glass of ice-cold orange juice, she took a long drink as she watched Tim's reaction to her question.

For a few seconds he didn't reply.

'Oh, come on, Tim! If you know something please tell me because if the money's not legal I don't want to have anything to do with it.'

'Of course it's legal!'

'Well, thank heaven for that! Then I really can accept it.' She leaned back in her chair. 'I feel so relieved that it's finally over. I'm going to put Rick out of my mind for ever.'

He reached across and touched her arm lightly. 'Do you really mean that, Katie? Can you finally put your relationship with Rick behind you?'

'Of course! Resolving the money question was the final obstacle to be removed and, as far as I'm concerned, that's been achieved.'

'That's what I hoped you'd say.' He paused. 'That's why I set this up.'

'Set what up?'

'The return of your money.'

'Tim, you've lost me! What...?'

He took a deep breath. 'Let me start at the beginning. A couple of weeks ago I got a registered package in the post. It was from Rebecca. It contained the diamond engagement ring I'd given her.'

'But what has the ring got to do with Rick paying back the debt?'

'There was a brief note from Rebecca, saying that she

was getting married. She wanted me to have the ring back.'

He stood up and walked over to the edge of the veranda, holding the railing as he gazed out to sea. For a few moments he was silent.

'And, do you know, Katie, it gave me an enormous sense of relief? My feud with Rebecca was finally over.'

He turned round to face her and she saw that his eyes were shining with excitement. 'Oh, I didn't care about the value of the ring. I've already sold it and put the money in an educational trust for Musa. It was—'

'You've put it in a trust for Musa?' she said. 'What a wonderful idea! But if you didn't want the ring why was it so important to get it back?'

'Because it restored my faith in human nature. I realised that I couldn't go on hating Rebecca. It was poisoning me—emotionally that is. I had to move on...to the next relationship in my life.'

He came across and held out his hands. 'Do you know what I'm trying to say?'

She swallowed, not daring to hope. 'You'll have to explain.'

He pulled her to her feet and held her gently against him.

'After Rebecca cheated on me I thought I could never love again.'

Light was beginning to dawn. 'I felt the same after Rick.'

'It was like a release from prison when the ring arrived. I knew that if only I could engineer the same sense of relief in you then we would both be free to make a real commitment to each other. I sensed that you were still being emotionally poisoned by the grudge you were carrying against Rick.'

She pulled herself away so that she could watch the deep intensity of his expression. Standing at arm's length, she quietly asked him how he'd managed to engineer the return of her money.

'It's a long story. Let's go inside into the air conditioning. I'm getting too hot out here.'

He took hold of her hand and steered her towards the veranda door. Closing the door behind them, he drew her with him towards the bed.

'Tim, I'd like to be able to concentrate on your explanation,' she told him, as his arm encircled her waist to pull her onto the bed beside him. 'If you're holding me...'

'It will be easier to explain if we're both comfortable.'

She leaned against him, trying to ignore the tremors of physical desire that his proximity aroused in her.

'As you know, I often dive with Rick. Last month, when we were having a couple of beers after our dive, he told me he'd had a letter from his grandmother's solicitor, saying she'd died and left him some money.'

'I didn't know he had a grandmother.'

'Neither did he until he got this letter from her solicitor. Apparently, she'd disowned his sixteen-year-old mother when she became pregnant, but she'd asked her solicitor to keep track of her only grandson. She was quite happy to ignore him during her lifetime, but wanted to leave him her money after she died.'

'He must have been over the moon!'

'He was. Anyway, when Rebecca sent my ring back I got to thinking that you'd find the same sense of relief if Rick paid you back. So I showed him the figures concerning his debt that you'd given me. At first he argued that he wanted to pay you back in instalments, but I persuaded him to arrange a transfer of funds for the whole amount, and hey presto! You're completely cured of the deadly can't-love-again disease...I hope!'

She turned her head to look at him. 'I've been cured for some time now. You were the one who was always insisting you could never love again and—'

'But you'd been so insistent that... Oh, Katie! If I'd only known!'

He cradled her in his arms, nuzzling his mouth against her hair until his lips found hers in a long, tender kiss.

'I tried so hard to dampen my feelings for you during the time I was away in New Delhi,' he told her when they both came up for air. 'I felt I didn't have the right to try to get serious. You seemed relieved when I suggested we keep the relationship light and casual.'

'I was furious!'

'But why didn't you say so?'

'You'd been so insistent that Rebecca had put you off love for the rest of your life.'

'I thought she had...until I met you,' he said, his voice tender and husky with emotion. 'Will you marry me, Katie?'

The room was spinning. 'Tim, this is too much to take in all at once. I thought you wanted me to go back to the UK and—'

'It was hell every time you spoke about it! Look, I know marriage is a big step. I can wait for your answer but don't go back to the UK, Katie. Your contract can be extended. Stay out here until you've made up your mind.'

'I'm absolutely sure I want to marry you,' she heard herself say. It was like a dream come true. Any minute now she would wake up.

He took her face in his hands and kissed her gently on the lips. His fingers caressed her bare shoulders as he pulled her against him. A tantalising desire to be part of him again welled up inside her, and when his tender caresses became fiercely passionate she strained against him, striving to reach their ultimate moment of ecstasy.

Katie opened her eyes and stirred in Tim's arms as she watched the moonlight casting shadows through the louvred windows.

'How long have we been asleep, Tim?'

'Mmm… Does it really matter?'

She pulled herself out of his arms and sat up. 'We need to be practical for a little while. What about the poor candidates who are queueing up for my job?'

He propped a pillow behind his head.

'That won't be a problem. When I was at the New Delhi conference I put forward the idea that more islands needed doctors in residence, and my suggestion has been taken up. From now on doctors won't be appointed to a specific island. They'll move around between the islands, wherever they're needed.'

She smiled. 'You've thought of everything, haven't you, Dr Fielding?'

'Oh, we aim to please, Dr Mandrake.' He was reaching for her again.

She snuggled against him. She'd never been happier in her entire life. The dream hadn't ended. It was only just beginning…

EPILOGUE

'I HOPE you're not going to desert me tonight like you did last Valentine's Day,' Tim said, as he looked across the table at Katie.

She smiled. 'I've got to be back in hospital early tomorrow on Kamafaroo but I think I might be able to spend the night with you here in Male.'

She looked out of the window at the twinkling harbour lights. 'I remember wondering where I would be on Valentine's Day in a year's time. I never dreamed I'd be sitting here, in the same restaurant, at the same table…'

'With the same man,' he put in with a wry grin. 'An old married lady…'

'Less of the old! Thirty-one isn't old. You're forty!'

'And six months married to the same wife! Incredible! Is it because she's beautiful, talented, intelligent…?'

Katie laughed. 'All of those! Keep going. Flattery will get you everywhere tonight.'

She fingered the antique silver ring Tim had bought for her birthday at the same shop in Male they'd visited last year. It was of the same design as her necklace. Understated and exquisite, it didn't detract from her beautiful antique gold wedding ring.

'You said you had another surprise for me,' she prompted.

He leaned back against his chair, signalling for the waiter to bring coffee.

'I've taken a lease on that house you liked.'

'Oh, Tim! That's wonderful!'

Since their marriage they'd divided their time between Katie's water bungalow on Kamafaroo and Tim's medical residents' quarters in Male while they searched for a house. The beautiful old colonial-style stone house, situated in a large walled garden near the Male hospital, would be ideal for them. There had been problems in the negotiation for the lease and Katie hadn't dared to hope that Tim would succeed.

'We move in next month,' he told her. 'I can just see you, waiting for your husband at sunset on the veranda with a bottle of chilled wine, a couple of glasses and—'

'Or my husband, waiting for me to come over from Kamafaroo.'

He laughed. 'That's a possibility. But, seriously, darling, if you'd prefer to be transferred to Male I can arrange it.'

She hesitated. 'Not yet. I love Kamafaroo and intend staying there for as long as...as long as I can.'

His eyes narrowed enquiringly. 'What do you mean, as long as you can? If you're happy there—' He broke off and stared at her, a tentative smile lighting up his handsome features. 'Have you got a surprise for me?'

She smiled. 'There's no reason why I shouldn't keep on commuting until just before—'

'Darling! When is it due?'

He leapt to his feet and hurried round to her side of the table.

'I've only just found out. It's due in about thirty-six weeks. I did a test this morning and it was positive. Happy Valentine's Day, darling...'

'Your coffee, sir,' the waiter said.

'Bring a bottle of vintage champagne. We're going to have a baby.'

'Congratulations, sir! Your first?'

'Yes, but it won't be the last. We're hoping to have a large family.'

'The large family is news to me,' Katie said, smiling across the table as they clinked their glasses together.

He gave her a rakish grin. 'I thought we'd discussed it. Oh, well, we'll have to talk it over later tonight. It's not an unpleasant prospect, is it?'

'I've got nothing against the method of conception of babies.'

'Nor have I! Don't worry, darling, I'll help with everything. Conception, pregnancy, delivery…'

'Tell you what, Tim, why don't you have the baby and I'll do the delivery? Just think what a unique couple we'd be if we could arrange that!'

He put down his glass and reached for her hand across the table. 'I think we're pretty unique as we are…'

MILLS & BOON®

*Makes
any time
special*

*Enjoy a romantic novel from
Mills & Boon*®

Presents™ *Enchanted*™ *Temptation*.

Historical Romance™ *Medical Romance*™

MILLS & BOON®

Medical Romance™

COMING NEXT MONTH

All these books are especially for Mother's Da

* * *

A HERO FOR MOMMY by Jessica Matthews

Dr Ben Shepherd was unprepared for the impact Kelly Evers and her five-year-old daughter Carlie would have on his life...

BE MY MUMMY by Josie Metcalfe

Jack Madison's small son Danny was a delight, and he and Lauren were very drawn to each other. But why does this make Jack edgy?

MUM'S THE WORD by Alison Roberts

Dr Sarah Kendall anticipated a happy family life when she accepted Paul's proposal, but Paul's son Daniel had other ideas!

WANTED: A MOTHER by Elisabeth Scott

Adam Kerr needed a live-in nurse for his ten-year-old daughter Jeannie, but Meg Bennett was *so* much younger and prettier than he expected...

Available from 5th March 1999

Available at most branches of WH Smith, Tesco, Asda, Martins, Borders, Easons, Volume One/James Thin and most good paperback bookshops

MILLS & BOON®

Makes any time special™

Bestselling themed romances brought back to you by popular demand

Each month By Request brings you three full-length novels in one beautiful volume featuring the best of the best.

So if you missed a favourite Romance the first time around, here is your chance to relive the magic from some of our most popular authors.

Look out for
***Conveniently Yours* in February 1999 featuring Emma Darcy, Helen Bianchin and Michelle Reid**

FREE!

2 Books
and a surprise gift!

We would like to take this opportunity to thank you for reading this Mills & Boon® book by offering you the chance to take TWO more specially selected titles from the Medical Romance™ series absolutely FREE! We're also making this offer to introduce you to the benefits of the Reader Service™—

- ★ FREE home delivery
- ★ FREE gifts and competitions
- ★ FREE monthly Newsletter
- ★ Books available before they're in the shops
- ★ Exclusive Reader Service discounts

Accepting these FREE books and gift places you under no obligation to buy; you may cancel at any time, even after receiving your free shipment. Simply complete your details below and return the entire page to the address below. *You don't even need a stamp!*

YES! Please send me 2 free Medical Romance books and a surprise gift. I understand that unless you hear from me, I will receive 4 superb new titles every month for just £2.40 each, postage and packing free. I am under no obligation to purchase any books and may cancel my subscription at any time. The free books and gift will be mine to keep in any case.

M9EB

Ms/Mrs/Miss/Mr ....Initials...
BLOCK CAPITALS PLEASE

Surname ....

Address...

....

....Postcode ....

Send this whole page to:
THE READER SERVICE, FREEPOST CN81, CROYDON, CR9 3WZ
(Eire readers please send coupon to: P.O. BOX 4546, DUBLIN 24.)

DIANA PALMER

ONCE in PARIS

Brianne Martin rescued grief-stricken Pierce
Hutton from the depths of despair, but before
she knew it, Brianne had become a pawn in an
international web of deceit and corruption.
Now it was Pierce's turn to rescue Brianne.
What had they stumbled into?
They would be lucky to escape with their lives!

1-55166-470-4
Available in paperback from March, 1999